THE
Volcano
OF
Doom

Children's Books by
Sigmund Brouwer

FROM BETHANY HOUSE PUBLISHERS

THE ACCIDENTAL DETECTIVES

The Volcano of Doom
The Disappearing Jewel of Madagascar
Legend of the Gilded Saber
Tyrant of the Badlands
Shroud of the Lion
Creature of the Mists
The Mystery Tribe of Camp Blackeagle
Madness at Moonshiner's Bay
Race for the Park Street Treasure
Terror on Kamikaze Run
Lost Beneath Manhattan
The Missing Map of Pirate's Haven
The Downtown Desperadoes
Sunrise at the Mayan Temple
Phantom Outlaw at Wolf Creek
Short Cuts

WATCH OUT FOR JOEL

Bad Bug Blues
Long Shot
Camp Craziness
Fly Trap
Mystery Pennies
Strunk Soup

www.coolreading.com

Accidental DETECTIVES

THE
Volcano
OF
Doom

SIGMUND BROUWER

BETHANYHOUSE
MINNEAPOLIS, MINNESOTA

Published by Bethany House Publishers
11400 Hampshire Avenue South
Bloomington, Minnesota 55438

Bethany House Publishers is a division of
Baker Publishing Group, Grand Rapids, Michigan.

Printed in the United States of America

Library of Congress Cataloging-in-Publication Data

Brouwer, Sigmund, 1959-
    The volcano of doom / by Sigmund Brouwer.
       p.   cm. — (Accidental detectives)
Summary: While vacationing in Hawaii, Ricky Kidd and his friends find a
very expensive statue that was stolen from a Tokyo art show, and the
thieves know that they have it.
    ISBN 0-7642-2564-2
    [1. Robbers and outlaws—Fiction. 2. Friendship—Fiction.
3. Hawaii—Fiction. 4. Mystery and detective stories.] I. Title.
    PZ7.B79984 Vo   2002
    [Fic]—dc21   2002002812

SIGMUND BROUWER is the award-winning author of scores of books. He speaks to kids around the continent in an effort to instill good reading and writing habits in the next generation. Sigmund and his wife, Cindy Morgan, divide their time between Tennessee and Alberta, Canada.

For Olivia
and the sunshine
you bring into this world.

CHAPTER 1

In the pitch-black darkness of five o'clock on a Friday morning, I decided that a Hawaii vacation definitely should not include bobbing in a small fishing boat five miles from shore with sharks coming in from all directions.

But that's where I was.

Worse, for the previous half hour, oily chicken blood had been spreading in the water behind the boat to attract any sharks that didn't already know about the four of us humans dumb enough to be here, protected from mile-deep ocean only by a thin fiber glass hull.

Beep. Beep. Beep. I was so nervous, I clutched my boat seat at the slight sound. Then I realized the noise was only a global positioning system at the front of the boat. I tried to relax.

Beep. Beep. Beep. A GPS bounced signals off a satellite and could give our location anywhere on earth, accurate to within ten feet. Helpful, maybe, but I wasn't sure it was necessary to know exactly where I'd be when the sharks got me.

"Amazing." Dad's voice broke into the quiet of a warm breeze that rustled a flag on the boat. Although he sat less than five feet away with his hand on a fishing pole, it was so dark I barely saw the outline of his body. "From what I've read, all it takes is about one blood particle in a million for sharks to smell blood. If you cut yourself and fell in the water, all sharks within two miles would know about it and zoom in as if they had radar."

I didn't need to hear that.

"That's really good to know, Mr. Kidd," Mike Andrews answered my dad. Mike sat beside me. He had red hair that he barely covered with a New York Yankees baseball cap. He was my best friend. Nearly thirteen like me. Most of the time he spoke with a grin that could earn cookies from the grumpiest of old ladies. With our boat dropping and rising with the waves, this was not one of those times. I didn't hear any grin in his voice as he continued to speak. "I was about to put one of these giant fishing hooks in my arm and throw myself overboard, but now I've changed my mind."

"Chopped up chicken guts should be good enough for now," Dad said. "We'll save you for later if that doesn't bring in the sharks."

"Ha, ha." Mike said to him. Then Mike leaned over and whispered in my ear. "Your dad's not serious, right?"

I didn't answer. All I could think about was how dumb this was.

Earlier, Joseph Norbert, Dad's college buddy, had thrown out the chopped up chicken pieces to attract the sharks. The hearts and lungs of the chickens were in a small net dragging behind the boat.

While the guts—Norbert called them chum—began to seep blood in all directions, he had run giant fishing hooks through baitfish. Big baitfish. Back at home, we would be happy to catch fish the size of this bait. Norbert had hooked one baitfish for each of our four deep-sea fishing rods. He'd tossed the bait into the water, running line from the rods that rested by their handles in brackets mounted on the side of the boat. Attached to the fishing line, floating on the surface thirty feet above the bait, were hollow plastic buoys for markers, each about the size of a basketball. Each buoy had a bell that would tinkle when something moved it by pulling on the bait.

I squinted past the edge of the boat, trying to see those buoys. Still too dark. Not even the first rays of dawn were peeking over the mountains of the big island of Hawaii to the east of us. The only light came from stars and from the masts of a fishing trawler as it slid past us about a half mile away.

"We wouldn't get hit by a big boat like that, right?" Although it was too dark for Norbert to see my arm, I pointed at the trawler. It seemed to be getting closer.

Norbert laughed. "It's got radar. Just like my small boat. The pilot of that vessel knows we're here."

I relaxed. But only a little.

"Mr. Norbert, exactly how long is your boat?" I asked, unable to shake my worries.

"It's a twenty-six-footer," he said. Norbert and Dad had been roommates back in their college days fifteen years before. Norbert was short and barrel shaped. He had shaved his head bald, and it was deeply tanned because he lived in Hawaii all year long. Seeing Norbert beside my Dad was a big contrast. Dad was slimmer and taller with medium-length brown hair and a trimmed beard—with not much of a suntan. Norbert lived on the Big Island year round; we lived in Jamesville, thousands of miles away. A small, safe town. With no ocean or circling sharks. Which was where I wished I were right now. Or at least back at Norbert's beach house, safe on the shore of Hawaii.

"And some sharks can grow to thirty feet long, right?" I asked. "Like the one in the movie *Jaws*."

"Occasionally," Norbert said, his voice rumbling from his powerful chest. Any taller, and he could have been a professional wrestler. "And they can weigh over a thousand pounds."

I'd seen the movie *Jaws*. And now I wished I hadn't.

I could picture a shark longer than this boat. A thousand pounds. Maybe closing in on us as we spoke. *If it tried to knock us out of the boat . . .*

"So what happens if we hook a monster like that?" Mike asked, almost squeaking. He knew exactly what I was thinking.

"Relax," Norbert said. "In all my years of shark fishing, the biggest I've ever caught was a six-footer. It—"

He stopped abruptly as a bell tinkled. Behind the boat. In the dark, deep water.

I knew what that tinkling meant. Out there in the darkness of the night and the deepness of the black ocean, something big had just arrived.

Something so big it could pull the bait hard enough to shake the bell on the buoy.

The bell tinkled again.

And again.

CHAPTER 2

Shark fishing had sounded like an exciting idea the day before. But that was on the safety of the beach. With wonderful bright sunlight blazing from a clear blue cloudless sky.

All of us had arrived by air from Jamesville the day before, and this was our first full day on the beach.

All of us meant a big group of vacationers on Easter break from school. First there was our family. Mom and Dad and my younger brother, Joel. And someone brand-new to our family: Rachel, my baby sister. She was nearly a year old and had just learned to walk. Which meant trouble. On the beach, she looked cute in a waterproof diaper and a sun hat and smeared with sunscreen. But I knew she could disappear in a second, giggling as she wobbled away from us; we all watched her closely all the time.

With our family, of course, was Mike Andrews. Mom had suggested taking Mike because we had enough air mile points that it wouldn't cost any extra money. I knew there was more to it than that. Although Mom hadn't said anything about it, I guessed she wanted to cheer Mike up because he was having a rough time at home while his parents were in the middle of a trial separation.

Lisa Higgins was also with us. Like Mike, she was the same age as I was. Long dark hair and eyes as blue as a perfect September sky. Threw a mean fastball. And smiled prettily as she struck you out. Lisa was with us to help look after Rachel—Mom had told Dad that if he was taking the family to Hawaii, she wanted it to be a vacation for her, too.

The reason we were visiting Hawaii was Joseph Norbert. He was an Internet stock trader who lived in a big beach house and was finally getting married after years of bachelorhood. Dad had been invited to be the best man at the wedding in just over a week, and Norbert had invited all of us to stay with him.

The day before, when we were relaxing in the sun, Norbert had joined us on the beach and told us some great shark-fishing stories. When he'd mentioned he was going out early the next morning, Dad had asked three times for him to take us. Norbert had finally agreed to take us out at four o'clock in the morning.

Yesterday Mike and I had been so excited about shark fishing that not once had we stopped to consider what it might be like on a tiny boat floating on an ocean miles deep. Nor had we really imagined what it would be like to hook a monster that was extremely well equipped to make meals out of humans.

We had imagined only the excitement and adventure.

And had forgotten about what it might mean when the bell on the buoy actually began to tinkle.

Like it was doing now.

A white circle of light hit the water as Norbert aimed a flashlight at the noise in the darkness. Its light caught the dull gray surface of a buoy as it bobbed upward. Then the buoy dove down. At the same time my fishing rod bent almost in half, and line began to strip off the reel.

"You got one!" Norbert shouted. The gray buoy sped away from our boat, out of the range of Norbert's flashlight. "Let it run. The rest of you reel your lines in."

The line whizzed off the reel for another thirty seconds. Then it stopped.

"Take up the slack!" Norbert urged me as he reeled in his own line. Dad and Mike did the same with their rods. "It's coming back."

It?! The thing big enough to swallow a baitfish the size of my forearm was coming back? Take up the slack? What I really wanted to do was cut my line and let it go before it got near the boat.

Instead, I followed Norbert's instructions.

I reeled as fast as I could. Then *bang!* It felt like a piano had fallen and slammed into my fishing hook, pulling it down hard and fast. Whatever it was, it had turned the other way. I was glad that my fishing rod handle was supported by a bracket and that I was strapped to my seat.

"It's pulling our boat!" Mike shouted.

"Give it slack!" Norbert urged. "I'll get control of the boat. We've got to follow it before it breaks the line."

He handed the flashlight to Mike and jumped forward to start the motor.

I let it run again. Until the whizzing of escaping line stopped.

The boat motor whined quietly as Norbert guided us back and forth.

I reeled again. Let it run again.

In his excitement, Mike had unstrapped himself from his seat. He stood beside me, swaying with the boat as he played the flashlight on the surface of the water. All we saw were glimpses of the hollow gray ball whenever it was close.

Zing! More line tore off my reel.

I waited until the run stopped, then frantically brought in the line again.

I realized I wasn't afraid any more. I realized I really wanted to catch this shark. I imagined myself at the wharf as Dad took a photo of me with the shark. I imagined telling everyone back at school what it had been like. I imagined a necklace of shark teeth, just like the ones I had seen in souvenir shops.

Zing! Another run. But it was slightly shorter than the one before. The shark was getting tired!

I reeled again. The fishing trawler had moved closer to us, but I didn't care. Norbert had told me it had radar. It wouldn't hit us. And I wanted to catch this shark.

The shark moved in and out. We went back and forth for fifteen minutes as Norbert moved the boat to stay with the shark. My arms ached. My back ached. But I wanted to catch this shark so badly that I knew I wouldn't give up for anything.

Besides, I could tell it was getting more and more tired, too. I told myself I *would* catch it. It would be worth the pain and effort and aching muscles.

Zing!

As fishing line stripped off my reel, the global positioning unit began beeping like crazy. Louder and louder, more rapidly each second.

Beep! Beep! Beep! Beep! Beep! Beep! Just as if it were a heart monitor measuring the excited beats of my own heart.

My fishing line stopped whizzing as the shark made a turn back toward us. I ignored the beeping sound of the GPS as I concentrated on reeling hard and taking up the slack again.

The beeping continued, growing even louder and more intense, with the beeps coming faster and faster. I kept reeling.

"Nearly there!" Mike shouted, standing beside me, the nylon of his life jacket rustling against mine. "Nearly there!"

The boat turned sideways. Mike's flashlight showed that the gray buoy was almost back to the boat. Would we get our first look at a shark big enough to drag the boat?

Then, without warning, the flashlight beam shot upward.

Mike yelped and fell sideways. He yelped again as he tumbled over the edge of the boat. Into the darkness of the night. Into the darkness of the ocean.

With a shark closing in fast.

CHAPTER 3

Later that morning when Mike reached me on the beach, his shadow fell across my face.

"You've got to believe me," Mike said. He wore beach shorts and a Hawaiian shirt. When he wore Hawaiian shirts in Jamesville, they seemed out of place. Here, for the first time in his life, the shirt didn't look crazy on him. His New York Yankees cap put his freckled face in shade. "It wasn't an accident."

"You're blocking the sun," I said. I had taken off my own T-shirt. I sat in a beach chair with a book in my lap, wraparound sunglasses perched on my nose.

Mike didn't move. He crossed his arms across his chest. A small video camera hung from a strap around his neck. "How long are you going to stay mad at me?"

I looked past him at the blue ocean stretching to the horizon, then up and down the beach at all the other people on towels or in chairs. Lisa was back at the beach house supervising Rachel as she napped. Nearby were Mom and Dad. My younger brother, Joel, was in the water, knee deep, wearing a cheap snorkel set. In the swell of the waves, he could barely keep his balance in his flippers as he tried walking. Rock and roll music drifted softly toward me from Dad's portable CD player.

"How long are you going to stay mad at me?" Mike asked again.

I didn't answer Mike's question. I lifted my book and began to read about a girl named Scout and a trial in the South where a black man was unfairly accused of a crime. It was a great story. I would have read *To Kill a Mockingbird* even if it weren't a homework assignment to finish during this school vacation.

Mike repeated his question one more time. It was obvious he wasn't going to go away.

"Mad at you?" I said. I kept my eyes on the pages of the book. Some of the ink had blurred from suntan lotion smeared off my fingers. "Why should I be mad at you?"

"That's just it," Mike said. "You shouldn't be mad at me. I didn't fall out of the boat. I didn't jump out just to stop you from catching a shark. I told you. I was pushed."

I didn't look up from my book. "Yes. You told me as soon as we hit shore at six this morning when you knew Norbert couldn't hear you. You told me in my room after your shower. You told me after breakfast at eight o'clock. I bet I've heard you tell me a dozen times already. You were pushed. Norbert decided to throw you into the ocean."

"I didn't say he threw me. All I know is he bumped me hard enough to knock me out of the boat."

"Yes. I believe you."

"You don't believe me. I can tell by your tone of voice."

"Of course I believe you. He's a murderer, Mike. We should call the police and tell them he tried to kill you in front of two witnesses. But after trying to murder you, he quickly changed his mind. That's why he dove in after you and rescued you even though there was a shark somewhere nearby. All of it makes perfect sense to me."

Mike sighed. "Sarcasm is not pretty, you know."

"I'll tell you what I know. I know I almost had a shark. I could have gone back to Jamesville at the end of this Easter vacation with a photo of the shark and me. I could have had a set of shark teeth. Maybe made a necklace from it. But no. Just when I've almost won the fight with the shark, you get excited, lose your balance, and fall out of the boat. So Norbert has to cut my line, then jump in after you. Instead of pulling a shark in, we pull in one wet red-headed kid."

"I didn't fall out. I was——"

"And, if you keep standing there blocking the sun," I finished, "you are going to seriously wreck my chances of going home with a suntan, too."

Mike sat down beside my chair. With both hands, he dug into the sand. He lifted sand and let it fall as he spoke. "We've got nine days left on this vacation. Except now my best friend doesn't want to hang out with me. I didn't fall out of the boat by accident. What's it going to take for you to stop being mad at me?"

I shut my book.

"It's going to take you telling me the truth," I said. "People make mistakes. I am glad you weren't drowned or ripped apart by a shark. If you had just apologized instead of making excuses, I'd probably laugh about all of this. But when you blame Norbert—"

"So all I need to do is say that it was totally my fault and that I am very sorry for costing you a chance at catching a shark."

"This is Friday, the last day of March."

"Meaning . . ."

"All it's going to take is an apology and we can get back to planning our April Fool's stuff for tomorrow. We'll be buddies again."

Mike stopped sifting sand through his fingers and brushed them off against his shirt. He lifted his video camera and panned the water, taking in all the swimmers in front of us and the horizon where the ocean ended against the sky.

"Pretty, isn't it?" he said. "When I get home, I'm going to download this to my computer and watch it over and over again. I can sit in school and pretend I'm back here on the beach."

I didn't reply. I waited for his apology.

He must have known it. He stopped videoing and lifted his cap.

"See this?"

I nodded.

"Red hair. Something that stubborn people have. Like me. I can't lie. Not even to stop you from being mad. Because now it's making me mad that you won't believe me. Your best friend."

I opened my book and pretended to read again. If Mike

was going to be stupid about all of this, I'd rather spend my time alone on the beach.

Mike caught the hint. He stood so quickly that his video camera bounced off his chest.

"See ya," he said.

"See ya," I replied. I could be just as cool as he was.

He started to walk away.

"Mike," I said.

He stopped and turned. "Yeah?"

I should have remembered that he was trying to pretend it didn't bother him that his parents were probably getting divorced. I should have reminded myself that he and I had been best friends forever. And I really shouldn't have ignored the sudden and eager grin on his face, like he was hoping that I would say it was all right, that I wasn't mad at him any more.

But all I thought about was his dumb excuse about being pushed out of the boat. How it had cost me a shark.

"I don't know where you're going," I said. "But do yourself a favor. Make sure you don't fall into the ocean again. I doubt Norbert will be around to rescue you this time."

His grin faded. He tried to hide the hurt in his face.

"Sure," he said, tightening his lips. "I'll do that."

He turned again and walked away from me, keeping his shoulders straight with pride. He walked down the beach toward the small marina where Norbert kept his boat docked.

I tried to read my book.

I couldn't. I thought of the hurt on Mike's face. I tried

to tell myself that he was the one who owed me an apology. I tried not to think about something else, too. That I
believed in God and that because of it, I wanted to follow
Jesus and His example. That if I really wanted to follow
Him, it meant reaching out to others, even when I didn't
feel like it. And forgiving. Mike hadn't asked me to forgive
him because he was too stubborn. But I knew him well
enough to understand that. So maybe, difficult as it was, I
should tell Mike it was okay.

I shook my head at myself. If it was this tough to forgive a best friend, how much tougher to forgive people
who didn't like you. At least I wasn't facing that right now.

I closed my book and stood up to go looking for Mike.

That's when an older lady knee-deep in the water
nearby began to jump up and down and scream as if a
shark had grabbed her by the leg.

I looked over and groaned.

Joel . . .

CHAPTER 4

Dad got there first.

Almost.

As Dad ran from his beach chair into the water toward the woman, a small kid surfaced from knee-deep water and Dad had to dive sideways to miss. Dad belly-flopped with a gigantic splash.

I jumped over Dad's spread-eagled body.

"Joel!" I had to yell to be heard above the screaming of the woman. She wore a black one-piece bathing suit and clutched a straw beach hat to her head with one hand, pointing at Joel with the other.

More accurately speaking, she pointed at an eel draped across Joel's shoulders and arms.

"Joel!" Dad had caught up to me. By now I was sure everyone on the beach was staring at us. The woman kept screaming.

Below his diving mask, Joel smiled his innocent smile. Joel didn't speak much, so I wasn't going to waste time asking him why he had decided to show his prize to this woman. His brown hair was soaked to his head. The eel around his neck did not move.

I knew why.

It was dead. Only my six-year-old brother would play with a dead eel. Only he would proudly show it to the nearest adult.

I reached for the eel. It felt like a slimy rope. I pulled it from Joel's neck.

"Sorry," I said to the lady as the eel dangled from my hand. "He must have found it floating nearby."

Then I began to scream.

The eel had flopped suddenly and tightened itself on my arm. As I tried to shake it loose, it snapped its head sideways and bit into my stomach.

"Aaagh!" I shouted. "Aaagh!"

I ran as fast and as hard as I could, trying to shake it loose.

"Aaagh!"

I tripped in shallow water and fell face forward. My head banged into the sand. I rolled over and got to my knees.

The eel was gone. Probably headed for deep water to get away from all the commotion.

I stared at my stomach. There was a dull red mark where the eel had bitten. Its teeth had not punctured my skin. That was the good news.

The bad news was that everyone on the beach was staring at me. And that my nose was plugged with sand.

I coughed out a mouthful of seawater and blew my nostrils clear, spraying sand in all directions.

That's when I noticed a Japanese tourist filming all of this with a video camera.

I waved weakly in his direction.

Welcome to Hawaii, I thought.

I'd lost a shark. Driven away my best friend. Been attacked by an eel. And suffered public embarrassment.

At least, I told myself, *it can't get worse.*

Right?

CHAPTER 5

"Richard."

I looked up at Lisa. After the eel I'd gone back to Norbert's beach house because I didn't like people pointing at me and whispering and giggling. Lisa and I were on the deck at the back of the house. She sat in a beach chair with my baby sister, Rachel, asleep in her arms. Lisa's lips were tight as she repeated herself.

"Richard."

When Lisa called me by my full first name, it wasn't a good sign. Was Rachel's diaper full? Did this mean Lisa wanted help changing it?

"Nice view, huh?" I said to Lisa. The mountains of Kona looked down on us, patched with the green of distant coffee plantations. The sky was bright blue with small white clouds drifting slowly, as if they, too, were on vacation and in no hurry to go anywhere.

"Richard."

"Thirsty? I know you're busy with Rachel, so I'll run inside and get you some lemonade."

"Don't move," she said.

Rachel's little blond head was tilted back against one of Lisa's arms as she snored softly. Who knew little babies could snore?

I cautiously sniffed the air but didn't smell anything from Rachel's diaper. Maybe I was safe.

"I want to talk to you about Joel's homework," Lisa said.

Suddenly I wasn't so safe. "Hey, speaking of Joel, did I tell you about the eel he found a half hour ago? Mom and Dad and I were on the beach. I was reading a book, minding my own business, and somehow, he manages to grab an eel."

I talked quickly so she couldn't break in. "You know how Joel has this thing with wild animals. I mean, wild squirrels will come up to him and eat out of his hand. And you remember the time we were camping and he found a bear cub. Well, this was like that, except not quite as bad. Eels don't have mothers that chase you up a tree, right? So somehow—maybe the eel was half dead anyway—he's snorkeling and comes up with it around his shoulders and for some reason it doesn't bite him even though it was happy enough to bite me later. Anyway, he shows it to a woman and she—"

"Richard." She cut me short with a glare. "I saw you and Mike helping Joel with his homework on the airplane. Didn't I? And you both giggled a lot as you helped him."

"Heard from Mike?" I said. "He took off and I haven't seen him since. Maybe I should go try to find—"

"Richard. The four seasons, I believe, are winter,

spring, summer, and fall. Would you agree?"

Busted. I tried to wiggle out of this anyway. "Maybe not if you're cooking."

"What are the four seasons? That was one of Joel's homework questions. Any idea why he answered with salt, pepper, mustard, and vinegar?"

"It was only a suggestion." I coughed. "Mike's suggestion."

Lisa reached underneath her beach chair. She pulled up a paper and read aloud from it. I recognized the paper, of course. It had Joel's handwriting.

"Here's one of his science assignments." Lisa cleared her throat and read. "Dew is formed when sun shines down on leaves and makes them sweat."

"Did you notice that we helped him spell all the words correctly? Think of the extra points he'll get for that."

She ignored me and kept reading aloud. "The body consists of three parts. The brainium, the borax, and the abominal cavity. The brainium contains the brain. The borax holds the heart and lungs. And the abominal cavity contains the five bowels: A, E, I, O, and U."

"It was a long flight," I protested. "It was getting boring and—"

"And I'm sure you're going to spend a little more time this week with Joel on his homework, right? Like maybe helping him with the correct answers."

"You sound like my mother," I grumbled, not loudly enough for her to hear.

"What did you say?" she asked.

"Nothing," I said.

"If I sound like your mother," Lisa said, glaring again, "it's only to save you from what she'd say about this."

If Lisa heard me in the first place, why did she ask me to repeat myself? I shook my head. *Girls.*

"I know what that look meant," she said, hiding a grin. "You—"

Beside her chair, Lisa's walkie-talkie squawked. Lisa had an official baby-sitting service back in Jamesville, and one of the things that parents liked was that Lisa had a set of four long-range walkie-talkies. Jamesville was a small town; she'd give one to the parents and keep one herself and one for the kid so that they could communicate at any time. For this vacation, Lisa had brought all four.

"Lisa, come in." The walkie-talkie binged. That was a convenient feature of the walkie-talkie. You didn't have to say "out" when you finished and let go of the talking button. The bing let you know the person on the other end had released the button and was waiting for a reply.

"Lisa here."

"It's Mike." His voice sounded hollow coming from Lisa's walkie-talkie. I'd forgotten he had one clipped to his belt. I'd left mine in my suitcase. "I can't get hold of Ricky on his."

Lisa held down her Talk button and spoke clearly into the walkie-talkie. "Mike, I found it interesting that Joel thinks flirtation is one of the ways to make water safe to drink. Something about removing large pollutants like sand and canoeists and dead sheep."

There was a brief hiss of static.

"What's that?" Mike said. "Your voice broke up there."

"Nice try, Mike," Lisa said. "I know you're making that hissing sound yourself. You heard me. Joel's homework."

"Did Ricky squeal on me?"

"No. And watch what you say. He's right beside me."

"Good. I need you both to get here as soon as possible."

"I can't go anywhere. I've got Rachel and—"

"Hello!" My mom came around the corner. "Want some time to yourself, Lisa?"

"Hang on, Mike," Lisa said. "I'll get back to you in a minute."

"Perfect timing, Mrs. Kidd," Lisa then said. Mom hurried past me and gently took Rachel from Lisa.

Rachel didn't wake. She just kept snoring.

Mom waved good-bye as Lisa and I walked away.

As we got to the front of the beach house, with the ocean wide and blue in front of us, Lisa spoke into the walkie-talkie. "We're on our way. Where are you, Mike?"

"You know where the 24/7 convenience store is down here in the village?"

Lisa looked at me. I nodded.

"Yes," Lisa answered into her walkie-talkie.

"I'm hiding in a fern bush behind the store. Get here as soon as you can. It's very important."

CHAPTER 6

Lisa and I squatted beside Mike underneath a huge leafy fern. Ahead of us was the back of the convenience store. The front of it was set on a quiet street near the marina. On both sides of the store were tourist shops with souvenirs and disposable cameras and racks and racks of postcards that we'd checked out the day before.

"Mike," I said, "you stink."

"Hey," Mike protested. "I already know you're mad at me."

"No," I said. I sniffed the air. "I mean you really stink."

He did. It was a sour stink, like rotted vegetables and curdled milk.

"What's happening, Mike?" Lisa said. "We got here as fast as we could."

Mike pointed straight ahead, pushing aside some of the bright green leaves of the fern. "We need to find out who is going to show up at that Dumpster."

"Right," Lisa said. "Seriously, what's happening?"

"Shhh! The door is opening!" Mike pulled his hand back from the fern leaves. We all froze at his warning signal.

Mike lifted his video camera. He parted the leaves again and began to record the scene in front of us.

The Dumpster was dull orange, scraped up, and battered. One of the lids was wide open. As we watched, a man in a white uniform stepped out the back door of the convenience store. He carried a can of garbage to the Dumpster, heaved it upward, and emptied the contents inside. Then he walked away with the empty garbage can.

"Nuts," Mike said, ending the video recording.

"Nuts?" I said.

"Thought maybe this was the guy for the pickup."

"Pickup?" Lisa asked.

"But I was wrong," Mike said. "I guess that guy probably works in the store."

"Yeah," I said. "The white uniform with a 24/7 patch on the front is a dead giveaway. And the fact that he went in and out of the back of the store."

Lisa sighed. "Guys, I could be spending time on the beach. Not watching a Dumpster."

She sniffed the air. "And Ricky's right. Mike, you stink."

"Listen," Mike said. "Somebody's going to show up here soon to collect something from the Dumpster that somebody else left for him."

"Um," I said, breathing through my mouth to avoid smelling Mike's stinky shirt. "Could you say that in a way that makes sense?"

"I followed somebody here from the marina," Mike said. "A guy with a bunch of earrings and bleached white hair. He dropped a fishing buoy from Norbert's boat into the Dumpster. The only reason I can think of is that he left it for someone else to come by and pick it up."

"That's where you went after you left the beach?" I asked. "To watch Norbert's boat?"

"Not watch it. I was going to go on it and look around. But when I got there, the white-haired guy was on board. So I hung back and watched him steal the fishing buoy. I'm sure it's been prearranged for someone else to take it from this Dumpster."

Mike spoke with utmost seriousness. He was either unaware or didn't care about how crazy he looked, sounded, and smelled.

"Fishing buoy?" Lisa echoed. "I don't get it."

"It's like a giant bobber," I said. "Big, gray, round. We used them to fish for sharks this morning."

"I know what a fishing buoy is," Lisa said. "What I don't get is why Mike thinks one person would steal it and leave it here for someone else to take out of this Dumpster."

And I didn't get why Mike had gone to Norbert's boat in the first place.

Lisa sniffed the air again. She frowned. "Mike, you went *in* the Dumpster, didn't you?"

"Yes, and—"

Mike stopped as the rumbling sound of a truck's diesel engine reached us. Seconds later a garbage truck rounded the corner of the convenience store and headed straight to the Dumpster. The driver lowered forks to the base of it, and the hydraulics whined as the forks lifted the Dumpster up and over the truck. The Dumpster clanged as the driver emptied all of the garbage into the back of the truck. More whining of hydraulics as the driver set the Dumpster back in place.

The driver backed the garbage truck away and drove off.

"Well," I said to Mike. "This blows your theory right out of the water, doesn't it? If this was prearranged, you'd think the second person would have shown up in time."

"Not so fast, smart boy," Mike answered. He grinned. "I can give you one good reason I know something strange is happening."

"Sure," I said. "Just like you're certain Norbert pushed you out of the boat in the middle of the ocean."

"Lisa's right," he said. "I did go into the Dumpster. And that's why I have my one good reason. I found this inside the fishing buoy."

Mike reached inside his Hawaiian shirt. When he pulled his hand out, Lisa gasped.

Mike held a small statue of a Japanese warrior holding a sword extended chest high. The statue was studded with rubies and emeralds that gleamed in the noon sun.

Mike grinned at our shocked silence. "So what do you think about my theory now?"

CHAPTER 7

Half an hour later the three of us were on the beach. Lisa had the statue in the gym bag that she used to carry her towels and bottles of lotion and sunglasses and hat and whatever other stuff she managed to jam into the bag.

I had barely been able to wait this long.

"Mike," I said as we settled down on the sand. "You took forever in the shower to get rid of the Dumpster smell. You made me bribe you by buying a large milk shake. Now will you finally tell us what happened?"

"I'm not sure one milk shake is enough."

"Don't push me," I told him. "I may not be over the shark thing yet."

He slurped and burped and apologized and grinned. The beach was crowded with vacationers. On the water, a motorboat pulled a tourist on a parasail. Mom and Dad and Joel and Rachel were farther down the beach.

I waved at them.

Mom waved back. Joel didn't see us; he was

building a sand castle. Which was a good thing. If Joel wanted to hang around us, we wouldn't be able to talk freely.

"The shark thing," Mike said. "That's why I went back to Norbert's boat. I wanted to prove to you I really was pushed."

"Pushed?" Lisa asked.

"That's what I told Ricky all morning. I didn't fall overboard. Norbert pushed me."

"Norbert dumps you overboard and then rescues you," Lisa said. "Doesn't make sense."

"Which is why I didn't believe him," I added. "Until now."

Mike slurped again and sighed with satisfaction. "There was something else that didn't make sense when we were shark fishing. How much time Norbert spent looking for the buoy after he rescued me. Remember?"

I remembered. Just before jumping in for Mike, Norbert had cut my fishing line to set the shark loose. Norbert had dived into the darkness, splashing around to get Mike, who floated nearby in a life jacket. Dad had helped Mike and Norbert get back into the boat. Then Norbert had spent another twenty minutes guiding the boat in small circles as he looked for the buoy that had been cut loose.

"It just seemed weird to me," Mike said. "That he cared so much for the buoy. And I was desperate to prove to you that Norbert was up to something. So I decided to go back to the boat to look at the buoys. I had this crazy idea that maybe he stuffed them with drugs and he couldn't afford to lose them."

Mike stopped and caught the looks on our faces. "I know, I know," he said. "I watch too much television. But as it turns out, I wasn't so crazy after all, was I? Like I said before, I got to the marina and saw the guy already in Norbert's boat. I hid behind the hull of a sailboat and videoed what he was doing. He took a buoy and left on foot. He didn't go far because the Dumpster behind the convenience store was close by. After he dropped it in there, I dug it out. I found a small latch that opened the buoy, and inside, I found the statue. I put the buoy back in the Dumpster and called you guys by walkie-talkie. You know the rest."

"But if the white-haired guy was delivering the buoy by leaving it in the Dumpster," Lisa said, "wouldn't the next person have gotten there before the dump truck?"

"Maybe they didn't know the pickup schedule," Mike said.

I shook my head. "This seems so well planned. And the statue looks like it's worth a lot of money. I'm sure the people involved would have checked the schedule."

"Maybe the person picking it up got delayed," Mike said.

"And maybe we talk this over with your parents." This came from Lisa. "If the statue is worth any amount of money, they should know."

"I did think about that," I admitted. "But Norbert and Dad have been friends for so long. I'd hate to make it look like we were accusing Norbert of something that wasn't true. If we can just get a little more information one way or the other . . ."

Lisa didn't answer that. I took it as a yes.

"Back to more questions, then," Mike said. "Why would Norbert keep a statue in the buoy? And why risk it by fishing with it?"

I snapped my fingers. "He put it in the buoy because he was going to deliver it to someone. Mike, when Norbert was telling us about shark fishing, Dad had to really work hard to convince him to take us. Say you're Norbert and you want to drop the buoy off for someone else to pick up. You use shark fishing as an excuse to go out in the dark. You actually do the shark fishing so no one suspects anything. When the other person shows up by boat—say the white-haired guy—you give him the buoy. But Dad wrecked Norbert's plans by asking to go with him. Instead of making a delivery this morning, Norbert warned the white-haired guy we would be with him. That means the white-haired guy had to take it from the marina in broad daylight."

"Far too dramatic," Lisa said. "You've *both* been watching too much television."

"No, I'm with Ricky," Mike said. "What he says makes a lot of sense to me."

"Then why," Lisa answered Mike, "would Norbert push you overboard and cut the line loose? If Ricky's theory is right, the last thing Norbert would want is to risk losing the buoy."

Mike's grin faded.

As did mine.

"She's got us there," Mike admitted to me.

"And you guys have been pretty quick to assume

Norbert is part of this. What if he doesn't even know about the statue? What if the simple truth is that he just hated to lose the buoy and knew nothing about what was in it?"

"That brings us right back to why Norbert would push Mike overboard," I said. "That in itself is pretty suspicious."

Lisa and I both turned our faces toward Mike. We let our next question hang.

"Really!" Mike protested. "He *did* push me overboard. And remember, there is a statue here—from a buoy on his boat. So something is happening, even if we can't explain it."

More silence between us as we thought about this. The screaming of seagulls and the laughter of people on the beach filled that silence.

"Well then," Lisa said, "maybe we should start with the statue. If we know exactly what it is, that might answer a few other questions. Like how Norbert got it, who wants it, and why it had to be hidden."

"Exactly," Mike said, "I was just about to say that."

"Sure," Lisa smiled.

"Of course," Mike continued, "finding out what the statue is without letting anyone know we have it might be difficult."

"Not really," I said. "Let me give you one word."

They waited and I delivered with a smile.

"Ralphy," I said. I added more, even though they already understood. "Ralphy Zee."

CHAPTER 8

"Hey, guys! Hello from Jamesville. How is Hawaii?"

Ralphy Zee's face peered out at Mike and Lisa and me from the screen of my laptop computer. His computer, like mine, had a Webcam. Just a few minutes earlier I'd connected to the Internet and sent him an instant message online. It hadn't surprised us when he answered us within a minute. Although it was early afternoon in Hawaii, it was evening in Jamesville. Where else would Ralphy be but on the Internet?

"The weather is beautiful," Mike answered Ralphy's question. "We wish you were here. Or did I mean 'the weather is here and we wish you were beautiful'?"

"Hah, hah," Ralphy said. On my computer screen, Ralphy's eyebrows bobbed up and down, magnified by his large glasses. He and Mike and Lisa and I had been friends since kindergarten. In the fisheye view of his Webcam, his glasses seemed much bigger on his face than normal. His mouse-brown straight hair poked up in all directions, and I could guess that he sat in front of his computer, as usual, in a shirt that was wrinkled and way too big for him.

"There's something more than the weather," I said.

"Something else?" Ralphy's voice was slow and distorted from the slowness of the download. His mouth jerked open and shut as the pixels on the screen rearranged themselves.

"Not much time to explain," I answered. Mike and Lisa and I had hurried back to Norbert's beach house to connect to his phone line. We didn't know when he would return. And we didn't want Norbert to interrupt us. "Take a look at this."

Mike held the statue up in front of the Webcam of my laptop.

"What is it?" Ralphy's computer image asked.

"That's what we want you to find out if you can," Lisa said. "It looks Japanese."

A few seconds passed. We saw Ralphy push his glasses up on his nose, the way he always did when he was trying to think.

"Snap some photos of it with your digital camera," Ralphy said. "Download the JPEGs and attach them to an e-mail with as much information about it as you can. Since I'm on school vacation here, too, I'll have all day tomorrow to research it."

Ralphy grinned. He loved research.

"Done," I said. "We can't talk much longer."

"Talk to you tomorrow night, then. Same time."

"Gotcha," I said. His tomorrow night would be our tomorrow afternoon.

Ralphy waved good-bye. We waved back.

"I miss you guys," he said.

"We miss you," Lisa said. "Remember, we'll be back in Jamesville in a little over a week."

Later I'd think of Lisa's promise to Ralphy. And have reason to hope for it to come true.

CHAPTER 9

Anna Nichols was a tall, beautiful woman with long red hair that was partially covered with a white scarf so delicate it looked almost like a veil. She wore an elegant summer dress and lit up our breakfast table with a smile as bright as the engagement ring that Joseph Norbert had given her when he proposed.

We all sat on the back deck of Norbert's beach house. It was Saturday morning—the first of April—and the sky was just as blue as it had been the day before. A warm breeze tickled my hair. Hawaii was a great place for breakfast.

Anna Nichols had arrived only a few minutes before. It was our first introduction to Joseph Norbert's fiancée. Even with Mike and Lisa and Joel and I with the adults at the breakfast table, it was quiet. As if Anna was shy to meet all of us at once.

"Joseph." She broke the silence and handed Norbert the small box that she had brought out onto the deck with her. "I brought these doughnuts for you."

As if there wasn't already enough food at the table. Dad had made pancakes and poached eggs and grilled sausage. There was a pot of coffee, a few containers of orange juice, cereal, and bowls of fruit.

"Thanks, babe." Norbert opened the box, took one of the doughnuts, and dipped it in his coffee. He continued to speak as he brought the doughnut up to his mouth. "It was nice of you to join all of my friends this morn—"

He stopped halfway through his bite into the doughnut. A strange look crossed his face. He gagged, then spit the doughnut on the floor.

Rachel, in a high chair beside the table, clapped and giggled. It didn't surprise me. A baby her age would naturally approve of people throwing food on the floor.

"Honey?" Anna asked. "You don't like my cooking?"

He grimaced. "Of course."

Norbert attempted another bite of the doughnut. Once more he gagged and spit it on the floor. Once more my little sister clapped and giggled.

"April Fool's!" Anna grinned. "A Play-Doh creation."

"Play-Doh?" He rinsed his mouth by swigging down some coffee.

"Play-Doh. With food coloring. Gotcha, hook, line, and sinker."

Mike and I exchanged glances. This elegant woman had just played an April Fool's joke? I decided right then that I liked her. A lot.

I saw Mom winking at Dad. I knew that meant Mom liked her, too.

I was just about to play my April Fool's joke on Mike

when Mom asked Joel to get the suntan lotion.

"It's in my gym bag," Lisa told Joel. Joel disappeared into the house.

"Speaking of April Fool's," Dad said, trying to frown. "I had a very difficult time getting in my pants this morning."

"Difficult," Mom said. "You fell over."

"To me, that means difficult. It had something to do with someone sewing through each one of my pants legs."

Anna laughed.

"Mike?" Dad asked. "Ricky?"

We tried to look innocent.

"That's what I thought," he said. Then he grinned. "Of course, me falling down wasn't nearly as funny as your mom stepping out of the shower covered in purple."

"Not me," I said.

"Me," Lisa volunteered. "Kool-Aid in the showerhead. It's an old trick."

"Good one, Lisa," Mike said.

"Not as good as the rubber snake in my bed," she answered. "I nearly had a heart attack."

That was my April Fool's joke. But I wasn't about to admit it.

"Hey," I shouted. I pointed at the dark mountains behind us. "A lava eruption!"

Everyone turned.

"Very funny," Mike said. "What a lame April Fool's prank."

"Really," I said. I handed him a pair of binoculars. "Look for yourself."

"Sure. But I want you to know I don't believe it." Mike surveyed the mountainside for a few seconds, then handed me back the binoculars. "No lava. You didn't fool me for a second."

"You're too smart for me," I said, looking right into Mike's face and doing my best not to grin.

Earlier I'd put black shoe polish on the eyepieces of the binoculars. They had left round black rings around each of his eyes. He looked like a raccoon.

Mike heard all the giggles. "What?" he said defensively. "What did I do?"

Everyone laughed louder at his indignation.

In the middle of this, the phone rang.

"Ricky," Dad said, "can you go in and get that?"

"Sure," I said.

I tried to get up. And couldn't. I grunted and pushed harder. Still couldn't get off my chair.

"Hey!" I said. The phone kept ringing and Norbert stepped away to answer it.

Mom and Dad laughed. "April Fool's!" they said together.

"Super glue," Mike said. "Didn't you notice that they pulled up an old chair for you?"

I squirmed and pulled harder. Then heard a loud rip. I decided to stay where I was.

"Very funny," I said.

Actually, it was. Even funnier because Mike still had no idea that his eyes had black rings around them.

Norbert returned. Funny as it was to see Mike like a raccoon and me stuck to my chair with ripped pants,

Norbert didn't have much of a smile on his face. As he sat down, he spilled the container of cream on the table.

"Rats," he said. He stood quickly. "I've got to get more."

Once again he disappeared into the house but came back seconds later.

"Anna," Norbert said, "no cream in the refrigerator. I'm going to zip out to the convenience store and get some."

"Can't it wait?" she asked. "We were just starting to have some fun."

"I hate coffee without cream. I'll only be a minute."

At that moment, as Norbert opened the door to go inside, Joel stepped past him as he finally returned with the suntan lotion. But that wasn't all that Joel carried.

In his other hand, he held the small statue of the Japanese warrior.

"This was in Lisa's gym bag, too," Joel said. Norbert stood behind him, staring at Joel. "It's nice. Look at the jewels."

Like Norbert, we all stared at the rubies and emeralds in the statue.

And I waited for Norbert to start yelling at all of us.

Instead, he shut the door and walked away.

CHAPTER 10

A couple of hours later, Mike and Lisa and I sat in front of the Webcam of my laptop computer.

Ralphy's familiar face appeared on my screen.

"Aloha," I said.

"Aloha," he replied, his words slow and jerky, like the movement of his mouth. Even though the Internet was slower than talking by telephone, it was still nice for all of us to see him. "Has anyone rung your doorbell yet?"

"No," I answered. What a strange question. "Anything on the statue?"

"Well, I did get the e-mail and the JPEG. Pretty cool story about how you found it."

And strange that Norbert had pretended like it was no big deal that we had it in our possession. After he left at breakfast, Mike told Mom and Dad and Anna the truth. He'd found it in the garbage.

As for me, I'm glad I hadn't gone to Dad with accusations about Norbert. It seemed now—given that Norbert hadn't said anything when he saw it in Joel's hand—that Norbert was innocent of involvement.

But that didn't mean we were going to give up on trying to find out if the statue was as valuable as it looked, or why it had been hidden in a fishing buoy that some white-haired guy had stolen from Norbert's boat.

"The statue," Mike said impatiently. "I know it's a cool story. I was the one who found it. What I really want to know is what you know about it after a day of research."

"Well, I have bad news." Ralphy leaned forward, as if it could help him see us better. "Mike, get closer to the Webcam. There's something about your face. . . ."

Mike leaned forward.

Ralphy shook his head. "What is it, Halloween out there?"

"Halloween," Mike repeated. "Are you crazy? What does that have to do with our statue?"

"Mike," Ralphy said, "you—"

"The statue." I interrupted Ralphy before he could ask Mike about the black shoe-polish rings around Mike's eyes. Mike still hadn't looked in a mirror, and I wanted the April Fool's prank to last as long as possible. "What's the bad news?"

Ralphy blinked a few times, as if deciding whether to stick with the subject of Mike's raccoon eyes.

"The bad news?" I repeated.

"I'm not sure I want to talk about it," he said. "I'm afraid the police in Hawaii might already be on their way."

"What!" Mike nearly yelled. "Police!"

"If the doorbell rings at the place you're staying," Ralphy said, "you might not want to answer it."

"What!"

I rubbed my ear. Mike had yelled in it again.

"Sorry, guys," Ralphy said. "I found out on the Internet that the statue is a two-million-dollar museum piece stolen from an art show in Tokyo. I asked my dad what I should do, and he said we needed to contact the state police and get their opinion. When they found out about it, they immediately contacted troopers in Hawaii. Over the telephone, the troopers on the island demanded the address of where you are staying and—"

"Hang on," I said. The doorbell had just rung. "That might be them."

"I'm sure it is," Ralphy said. Ralphy brought his watch up and checked the time. He nodded. "When we spoke to them fifteen minutes ago, they said it would take about that long to get there. I told the troopers here that you are innocent, but it didn't seem like they believed me. I hope you don't spend much time in jail."

"Jail!"

I winced again at Mike's sudden shout.

The doorbell rang again.

"Ralphy," I said. "We'll get back to you. Okay?"

I shut down the computer as the doorbell rang a third time. Mom and Dad and Joel and Rachel had gone to the beach. Anna Nichols was out looking for Norbert, because even though a couple of hours had passed, he still hadn't returned from the convenience store.

"Police," Lisa said. "This isn't good. And what reason would they have to believe our story?"

"Two million dollars," Mike said, shaking his head.

"They'll lock us up and throw away the key."

We slowly made our way from Norbert's office through the hallway and to the front door of his beach house.

Once more the doorbell rang.

"I guess this is it, guys," I said. I wondered how many state troopers stood on the other side. "Hope they believe us."

I opened the door.

And looked into the eyes of a pizza delivery guy barely taller than I was. He wore blue jeans, a black T-shirt, and a baseball cap. Behind him on the road, engine running, was a compact car with the pizza company's sign on the side.

"Pizza," he said, "for Mike and Ricky and Lisa."

We were speechless.

"It's the strangest thing," he continued. "I mean, first of all, we don't get many pizza orders this early in the day. Second, the order came from some telephone number on the mainland. And I was supposed to deliver a message at the same time. So tell me, are you guys Mike and Ricky and Lisa?"

We nodded.

He handed us the pizza box.

"This pizza is from someone named Ralphy," he said. "I'm supposed to tell you I'm not the police."

I groaned.

"And one other thing," the pizza guy said. "He asked me to deliver this message, too. 'April Fool's!' "

I groaned again. "Anything else?"

"Yeah," the guy said. "It's fifteen bucks for the pizza,

and Ralphy promised that you'd give me a ten-dollar tip."

Wonderful.

Without warning, Mike bolted past the pizza guy, pulling me by the arms.

"The white-haired guy!" Mike shouted.

CHAPTER 11

With Mike yelling beside me, I half stumbled as he dragged me toward the street.

"It's him!" he shouted again. Mike pointed at the back end of a green sedan. "He's driving it! He was here! I'm sure I saw his face as he looked at us driving by."

The green car disappeared around a corner. Mike trudged back to the house, where the pizza delivery guy gave us a strange look.

"First time I ever saw anybody your age run away from pizza."

Mike gave him a half laugh. "I'd still be running if I thought I could keep up to a car."

"The green one?" the pizza guy asked.

"Yeah."

"What's going on?" the pizza guy asked. "I mean, he was parked just down the road when I drove up."

Did that mean that the white-haired guy had somehow found out that Mike had spied on him? And then found out where we were staying for our vacation?

"So what is it?" the pizza guy was saying. "Some kind of April Fool's joke?"

His words snapped me out of my thoughts.

"Actually," I said, "a little more than that. We're just trying to find out who he is."

"Hey," Mike grabbed my arm again. "I got an idea!"

I didn't like the sound of his voice. Like he had a crazy thought and was about to share it.

"Maybe you can help us," Mike said to the pizza guy.

"Me?"

"Yeah. The guy doesn't have much of a head start. Maybe you could take us in your pizza car and—"

"Not a chance. I've got a second job, and I have to be there in half an hour."

"Nuts," Mike said.

"But if you want to find the guy, just wander back down to the town. It's not like there are so many people around here that you won't see him again."

Mike nodded. "Sounds good. Thanks."

The pizza guy cleared his throat.

"His money," Lisa said. "Get him his money. He needs to go."

"Sure," I said. I took a step toward the inside of the house.

"And Ricky?" Lisa said.

I stopped.

"Don't forget his tip," she finished.

Somehow I'd find a way to make Ralphy pay for this.

We stood on the doorstep and watched the pizza delivery guy drive off, his little blue car leaving behind a cloud of black smoke.

"I'm going to wring Ralphy's neck," Mike said.

"How?" Lisa asked. "He's across the Pacific Ocean from here."

"Admit it, Mike," I said. "He got us good."

"Well, he's the only one," Mike growled. "And at least it wasn't as lame as your lava eruption thing that wouldn't have fooled a two year old."

I nodded. I could hardly wait until Mike looked in a mirror and saw his raccoon eyes.

"We might as well face Ralphy now and get it over with," I said. "Then we can ask him what he really learned about the statue."

"Are you kidding?" Mike said. "It's been at least two hours since breakfast, and this pizza smells great. No sense in letting it get cold."

"The guy didn't have a bad idea," I said fifteen minutes later on the front steps in the sunshine, overlooking the bay. We'd done our best to finish eating all of the pizza, but there were still a couple of pieces left.

"You guys are slowing down," Lisa said, clucking her tongue as she pointed at the last few pieces.

"Give me a break," Mike said. "We just had breakfast."

"Like I could forget," Lisa said. "What, ten pancakes each?"

"We need our energy," Mike answered. "Ricky and I've gotta look for a bad guy."

"Maybe we should split up when we get downtown," Lisa said.

"We?" Mike arched his eyebrows.

"Yes, we. Give me a description of the car and the driver. I can walk around looking for him just as well as either of you."

"But . . ." Mike stopped himself, as if suddenly aware that it wouldn't be smart to continue his thoughts out loud.

"But what? Were you going to make some remark about me being a girl?"

Mike coughed. "Lisa . . ."

"So you were!"

"I thought maybe you had to baby-sit," he said. Weakly. I knew he was doomed.

"Baby-sit! Baby-sit! Like that's all that girls are good for?"

"That's not what I meant," Mike stammered. "Just that you've been baby-sitting and . . ."

Again he stopped. Another mistake. When Lisa's mad, the best thing you can do is keep talking so she doesn't get a chance to get started.

"Tell you what," Lisa said. "I'm going to make you a bet in honor of April Fool's Day."

"What bet?" Mike instantly lost his look of fake innocence. He leaned forward with interest in his eyes. He was a sucker for any kind of challenge.

"Wait here." Lisa stood from the steps and marched inside. She slammed the door behind her.

"Good one, Mike," I said. "Good one."

CHAPTER 12

Lisa returned with a newspaper. She pulled the center page out and unfolded it, holding each top corner with each hand so that the paper flapped like a blanket in front of her.

"Here's the deal," she said. "I'm going to set this down on the floor. Flat and spread out. You and Ricky will stand on one side. I'll stand on the other."

"What did I do?" I protested. "He's the moron."

Something I noticed Mike didn't protest.

"You're best friends," Lisa said, hands on hips. "Birds of a feather hang together."

I remembered something that Dad had told me once. And he was only half joking when he said it.

Watch out, he'd warned me. *When one woman gets mad at one man, all the women around her get mad at all men.*

This, I guess, was a case in point. I'd never have suggested that Lisa wasn't capable of doing anything Mike and I could do. One, because it wasn't true; she *could* do anything we could. Two, because I knew it would make her mad. But here I was, facing her blazing eyes as if I'd actually said it.

"So we stand on one side of the newspaper sheet and then what?" Mike was already hooked by whatever challenge she'd throw at him.

"Mike," I warned. Lisa was not stupid. Whatever the bet was, Mike would lose to her.

Lisa smiled. "Then what? Then I stand on my half and laugh at you guys while you both do your best to push me off."

Mike snorted. "Like we wouldn't be able to do it."

"I'm here to say otherwise. If you succeed, I'll stay and baby-sit while you go looking for the bad guy."

"Get ready to change plenty of diapers," Mike said. "We're going to knock you off the paper and head right downtown while you spend the rest of the day baby-sitting."

"Mike," I warned again.

"Really?" Lisa said. Softly. Dangerously. "But if you can't knock me off the newspaper . . ."

She tapped her front teeth with her right forefinger as she thought.

She smiled again. "I've got it. You mentioned diapers? If you can't knock me off the newspaper in less than fifteen seconds, you both wear diapers when we go to the beach. Over your swimming trunks so that it looks like all you've got on is diapers."

"Embarrassing as that sounds," Mike said, "I'm not worried for a second."

"Mike," I warned.

"Are you chicken?" he asked me. "You hit her low. I hit her high. She's off the paper in less than five seconds."

"Sucking on a pacifier," Lisa said.

"Huh?" This from Mike.

"Diapers around your swimming trunks and sucking on pacifiers. Saying 'mama' every ten steps or less."

"I'll agree," I said. "As long as you pay me back for the pizza if you lose."

"Plus baby-sit," Mike said. "Let's make that clear."

"Deal," Lisa said.

"Deal," Mike said.

"Deal," I said.

Mike grinned and cracked his knuckles. "All right," he told Lisa. "Let's get started."

"Sure," she said. She stepped toward the front door. She opened it, pulling it toward her.

She dropped the newspaper across the doorstep, stepped back, and spoke as she gave the interior of the house a sweeping gesture with her right arm. "Gentlemen, go stand on your half."

We did, moving to the coolness of the air conditioning just inside the entrance of the house.

"Now you stand on your half and start counting," Mike said with a grin. "We'll try to be gentle about this."

He lowered his shoulders to push into her.

"Hands on my back to brace me, Ricky," he said. "Give me a good shove only if she's not off the paper in two seconds."

I stood behind him and put my hands on his back.

"Both of you," Lisa said. "Both feet on the paper. No part of your feet can be on the floor."

Mike and I looked down to make sure no parts of our feet touched the floor.

As we did, Lisa shut the door.

"All right," she said from the other side.

"All right what?" Mike asked loudly. We were both staring at the inside of the door.

"All right," she repeated, her voice muffled with the door between us. "I'm on my half of the paper. Start pushing. You have fifteen seconds."

Mike and I stared at each other. At first blankly. Then with horror as we understood how she had tricked us.

"No fair!" Mike banged the door with his fist. "The door's in the way."

"You never said I couldn't put the door between us," Lisa called. "Twelve seconds left."

She had us.

"Don't waste time arguing," I half shouted to Mike. "Push the door open. She'll fall off the paper then."

He tried the handle.

"She's holding it!" he said. "I can't turn it!"

"Ten seconds," Lisa said.

"We're dead," Mike whispered. "Keep trying the door so that she doesn't move."

He ran down the hallway to the nearby kitchen.

I jiggled the door handle, trying to get it to turn. Lisa didn't budge.

On the other side, in the sunshine on the front steps, Lisa laughed. "Five seconds!"

"No fair," I said.

"No fair that you're not so smart?"

I didn't have a chance to answer. Mike returned, rushing down the hallway with a pitcher of lemonade.

"If I have to wear diapers," he hissed, "at least she can wear this. As soon as she lets go of the handle, shove the door open."

Diapers. And pacifiers. And saying "mama" every few steps. It wouldn't bother me at all to see her soaked with lemonade.

Lisa's laugh reached us clearly even with the door between us. "Time's up. You guys will look hilarious in diapers."

"I'm ready," I answered Mike. "Get her good."

Lisa turned the handle and began to open the door. I hit it with my shoulder and popped it open. Mike flung the sticky lemonade over my shoulder.

Right into a tall, redheaded woman in a beautiful summer dress.

Lemonade streamed down her hair and face and the front of her dress. She blinked a few times.

"Um, hello," I said to Anna Nichols. "Guess we didn't expect you back so soon."

CHAPTER 13

After she cleaned up, Anna Nichols met us on the deck at the back of the house, where we had a view of the dark green mountains. In jeans and a shirt borrowed from Norbert, she smiled, telling us one more time that she understood what had happened.

"Besides," she added. "It will be worth it after Lisa tells me what it was like to see you guys in diapers on the beach."

I sighed.

"Don't forget the pacifiers," Lisa added. "And the calling out for 'mama.'"

Anna smiled again, but then it faded. "Did Joseph call while I was changing?" she asked.

"No," Mike answered. "But I can tell you that when he gets back, he's going to be some kind of grumpy."

"Why's that?" Anna said. Her face looked tired.

"About a half hour ago I opened the refrigerator to get some milk," Mike told her. "And I saw a new container of cream. He wasted a trip."

Anna bent her head down. When she lifted her eyes to us a few seconds later, I saw tears.

"That's just it," she said. "I was already at the store. They never saw him. I'm afraid Joseph used the cream as an excuse to run away from our wedding."

"There's got to be a better explanation," Mom said to Anna. Mom had returned ten minutes later from the beach with Rachel, who fortunately was asleep. "When Joseph invited us here, he sounded so excited about getting married."

"That was six months ago," Anna said. She stared at the mountains. "Since then . . ."

"Yes?" Mom said gently.

Mike and Lisa and I sat nearby. I wasn't sure if I wanted to be part of this conversation.

"Since then he has begun acting very strangely. I think it's because he made some bad investments in his Internet trading. Money worries have been driving him crazy. And no matter how many times I tell him that we still have my salary as a teacher, it doesn't help. He's a proud man."

Anna spoke to Mom as if we weren't there. "See this?"

Anna lifted her engagement ring. A huge diamond in the center sparkled in the hot Hawaiian sun.

"It's beautiful," Mom said. "There's another reason I can't believe he's run away."

"It's also fake," Anna said. "He doesn't know that I know. He has so much pride that even though it doesn't matter to me, he couldn't bear to give me a smaller ring with a real diamond. I needed it appraised for insurance, and that's when I found out."

"Still, running away..."

"He's put himself under a lot of pressure lately," Anna said. "Our wedding is in one week. Maybe he just decided he couldn't handle all the expense. There's catering. The banquet hall. The honeymoon. Photographer. Getting married costs so much and..."

"But running away sounds too drastic," Mom said. "There must be another explanation."

"He lied about needing something from the store. He didn't go to the store. And he hasn't come back. That makes me very worried."

Mom tried a smile. "I'm sure any minute now he'll return. And then he'll be able to explain everything."

Anna sighed. "Whatever it is, I love him. I'm going to stay here until he gets back."

It turned out to be a long wait.

By seven o'clock that night Ralphy had sent us three different e-mails to let us know that he still hadn't found anything about the statue.

And by seven o'clock that night Norbert still had not returned.

CHAPTER 14

By seven o'clock, though, Mike and Lisa and I had something else to worry about. It happened in the afternoon on the beach, in front of dozens of sunbathers. While Mike and I were in diapers...

"Mama," I said. The rubber of my pacifier tasted awful. "Mama."

Mike and I waded in waist-deep water. That way people couldn't see our diapers. And we made sure to face away from the beach so people couldn't see our pacifiers.

"Haven't we been out here long enough?" Mike called to Lisa. "It's been an hour. We still need to go downtown to look for the white-haired guy."

Lisa sat on a towel in the sand, reading a magazine. Mom and Dad and Joel and Rachel were at

Norbert's beach house with Anna as she waited and hoped for Norbert's return.

She didn't even bother to look up. "Not now. I want you on the beach where people can see you."

"Technically, we're *at* the beach. I'd say we've paid off our debt."

" 'Mama,' 'mama,' " Lisa said. "And get that pacifier back in your mouth."

Mike groaned.

"These wet diapers sure are heavy," I said to Mike. "I feel sorry for my little sister when she fills them up."

Mike didn't answer.

"Come on," I said, "you're not still mad at me for the shoe polish around your eyes."

Mike had finally noticed sometime after we'd finished eating the pizza. He'd chased me around the house, yelling, which only made me laugh louder.

"I'm over it," he said, "but look. . . ."

I took my eyes off the incoming waves. I followed the direction of his pointing arm and saw a man in a straw hat with a metal detector. The guy swept the wide round pad of the metal detector just above the sand. He wore a headset connected to the metal detector.

I knew how it worked. He would listen for beeps in the headset that told him about the presence of any metal. Then he'd sift through the sand and look for it. If he was lucky, he would find coins, not bottle caps.

"Think you can rent those things?" I asked Mike. "It would be fun to spend a few hours looking. Maybe you'd find more money than it cost to rent."

"Look closely," Mike said. Which I thought was dumb. I *was* looking at the guy. Otherwise why would I have mentioned renting a metal detector?

"Mike, I *am* looking at the guy." Beneath the straw hat, he wore wraparound sunglasses. I guessed him to be in his twenties. Maybe a bodybuilder. His white T-shirt covered a wide, heavily muscled chest. He wore cargo shorts over thick thighs. Nike shoes. And a tattoo of a devil with wings on his left bicep.

A wave hit us and knocked us over. A few seconds later we found our balance again. I wiped salt water off my face.

"Lisa," I called. "I lost my pacifier."

"Find it," she called back.

"Forget the pacifier," Mike asked. He pointed again. "Can you see his face? The metal detector guy."

"Sure," I said. At least the part of it that wasn't covered by the sunglasses and the shade from the wide straw hat.

"I think it's him." Mike took a step toward shore.

"Him who?" I asked.

"The guy with bleached white hair at the marina yesterday morning. The guy who took the fishing buoy from Norbert's boat and put it in the Dumpster. The guy we were going to look for this afternoon."

I should have realized it immediately. Mike was right! The guy in Mike's video had the same kind of build.

I took a step toward shore, too. By then the guy in the straw hat had almost reached Lisa.

"Mike," I said, "what if . . ."

The straw-hat guy stopped right beside Lisa. He bent over to talk to her. We were too far away, of course, to hear anything.

Mike ripped off his diaper and began to run. I got rid

of my diaper and followed. Except another wave from behind caught us by surprise and wiped us out.

By the time we got to our feet again, the straw-hat guy was no longer talking to Lisa. He was squatting beside her with a hand on her gym bag.

We began to run again. By now we were in knee-deep water and splashing hard.

As we got closer, the scene unfolded in front of us. And we couldn't do a thing.

Lisa grabbed the handle of her gym bag and pulled it away from him.

He yanked back.

She refused to let go.

He lifted his other hand to hit her across the head.

With her free hand, she threw sand in his face.

Now Mike and I were on shore, dashing at full speed, with maybe ten paces left to reach them.

We were close enough that I heard him yelp with pain as the sand hit his eyes. He coughed violently.

Mike got there first. He dove into the guy's shoulders, knocking him over. I was a close second, hitting the guy in the midsection.

It seemed like he rose with no effort. Mike hung onto his neck. I had both my arms around his waist. He threw us off like we were little puppies.

I hit the sand first, landing flat on my back. With a *woof,* I lost my wind. A split second later, Mike landed head first in the middle of my stomach.

I lay in the sand, spread eagled, unable to draw a breath.

Mike got up slowly.

I tried to roll over.

The guy was now running away from us, past startled tourists. He'd left his metal detector and his straw hat behind. His bleached white hair showed plainly in the bright sunshine.

"He's getting away," Mike said on his hands and knees. "Do something."

"Uuunnnngh," I said, rolling over. It was hard to talk with no air in my lungs. Worse, my stomach was sending a bad, bad message to the rest of my body. "Uuuunnnnghh."

At the parking lot at the far end of the beach, the white-haired guy jumped in a dull green four-door car that looked like any other rental car on the island. He shot gravel from his tires as he gunned it out of the parking lot.

An older tourist stopped by. He had a belly like a beach ball and his skin was painfully red from sunburn. "Do you guys need help?"

"It's okay," Mike said. "We kind of know the guy."

The older tourist snorted before walking away. "Well, he sure plays rough if you ask me."

No kidding, I thought. My stomach wobbled with queasiness.

Lisa knelt beside us. "You guys all right?"

" 'Course," Mike said. "Did you see how fast he ran once he realized we had him whipped?"

"Sure," Lisa said. "Ricky?"

"Uuuunnnggggh." This was not a good feeling.

"He tried to buy my gym bag off me," Lisa said.

"When I told him no, he got pretty mad."

"Uuuuuuunnnngh?" I said. I was trying to ask if she still had the Japanese warrior statue inside it.

"The gym bag's got the statue, doesn't it?" Mike asked, standing and slapping sand off his body.

"Yes."

"Uuuuuunnngh." At least that question was answered. Now I was trying to tell them both to give me room. I thought of a lava eruption and felt even worse.

Lisa took one of my hands and tried helping me to my feet. I didn't have the energy to stand, and I was too heavy for her. I fell back onto my hands and knees. Our diapers washed up onto the shore nearby.

"Uuuuuunnnngh." There wasn't much time until . . .

"How could he know the statue was there?" Lisa said to Mike. "Even if he saw you go in the Dumpster for it, he couldn't know we were friends. And even if he did, how would he know the statue was with me in the gym bag instead of back at Norbert's beach house?"

"Uuuuuunnngh."

"Ricky," Mike said, "That sounds disgusting. Exactly what are you trying to tell us?"

I didn't answer. But my stomach did.

Mike had the misfortune of being the one closest to me. As I threw up, I hit his legs and his feet.

There was stunned silence for only a moment. "Gross," Mike said, throwing sand on himself to cover up the former contents of my stomach. He bent over and took a closer look. "Lisa, does that look like pepperoni from the pizza that Ralphy sent to us this morning?"

Lisa crossed her arms and glared at him.

"Thanks," I said weakly, "I really needed to hear that. Why don't you just go jump in the ocean?"

"Good idea," he answered. "Keep the statue safe while I'm gone."

As Mike walked away, Lisa spoke to me quietly.

"I hate to say this," she told me, "because I know that your dad and Norbert are old college buddies."

"Hate to say what?" I asked.

"There was someone in the passenger seat of the green car that the white-haired guy drove out of here." Lisa paused. "If I didn't know better, I'd say it was Norbert."

CHAPTER 15

"It's the strangest thing," Anna said. The clock showed seven. Darkness had fallen on the island. All of us sat in the kitchen. The remains of our barbecued hamburgers were on the table. "I can't find my white scarf. I had left it out to dry after washing lemonade out of it."

Mom and Dad and I looked at Joel. Usually he was to blame for anything unusual. Once I'd seen a turtle in our backyard wrapped in one of Dad's mitts; Joel had been afraid it might get cold.

"Not me," Joel said. "Some other guy."

"Some other guy," Mom said. "A real guy? Or an imaginary guy?"

Joel had a lot of imaginary friends. Including a dragon fighter and a cowboy.

"Real guy. I saw him leaving the house with the scarf."

Anna looked worried. "I fell asleep on the couch in the living room with it right beside me on a coffee table. If Joel is telling the truth, that means . . ."

She didn't have to say it. That meant the

intruder had walked in while she was sleeping and stolen it in broad daylight. With Mom and Dad on the back deck. That was bold.

"What did he look like?" Dad asked Joel. If Joel said anything about a cowboy hat or knight's armor, then it was an imaginary friend.

"White hair." Joel said. "Big, big muscles."

Mike and I cleared the table of all the dirty dishes. We met Lisa outside.

Above us, the stars were so bright they seemed to shimmer against the black velvet of the sky.

"I'm going to say something that a million people have already said," Mike told me.

"Yeah?"

We eased into chairs on the deck. The sun had set about an hour earlier, but it was still warm. A gentle breeze brushed at my hair. Hawaii was definitely a nice place to be.

"The stars," Mike said. "They're awesome. The sky is so clear and dark, and it seems like I could just reach up and touch them. Sure makes me think of God."

"Me too," Lisa said.

"Me too," I said.

There was a pause as we all quietly stared upward.

I spoke to fill the silence. "Ralphy was telling me some

physics stuff one day. That scientists ran a computer pro-gram to experiment with creating a model of the universe where the force of gravity was different or the force of the nuclear bonds of elements was different than in our uni-verse. Even the slightest of changes—like one thousandth of one percent—made the program construct models of universes incapable of supporting life as we know it."

"Ricky," Lisa interrupted. "If there's ever a day when you're older and with a girl and you're holding hands and both looking at stars on a romantic night . . ."

"Yes," I said.

"Maybe keep those thoughts to yourself. It kind of spoils the mood."

"Really," I protested. "It was interesting to hear Ralphy explain it. See, there are four fundamental forces of phys-ics, and if any one of them were at all different in the slightest way, no life. It's such an amazing balance that the odds of it happening by chance are mathematically impos-sible. Then there's other stuff. Like the fact that the Earth is exactly the right distance from the sun to support life. Ralphy says that some respected scientists are prepared to argue a theory from these facts that the whole purpose of the universe is to support human life. In the way that Gen-esis tells us."

"I just wanted to look at the stars," Mike said. "Not sit in on a university lecture."

"Lecture? But the science behind all of this is amazing." I paused. The stars *were* incredible. Like the beauty of the island. And the fascinating life in the ocean waters. Pretty easy to believe that God was behind it all.

"Of course," I continued. "It's not that Genesis explains all of this in scientific language. And that's the problem, right? That people try to use the Bible as a science manual to explain how the world was made, instead of as a way to explain why."

"Thanks, professor," Mike said.

Why the world was made. What a question. I thought it was cool that we now knew enough about science to understand it could point us to God. As much as biologists know about the human body, they can't explain love or art or conscience. All the invisible things that result from having a soul. And the reason why we were created was for our souls to have a relationship with God.

I kept staring at the sky. "In fact," I said, "many astronomers look at all the evidence and can't help but see God. Science gives them faith. To them, looking at the sky is like looking back in time. You see, light travels at about 186,000 miles per second. Which is fast, but the universe is so big that some of the starlight now hitting our eyes has been traveling across the universe for thousands of years to reach us. A star may have exploded a hundred years ago and be gone from space, but we won't know it until the light from the explosion finally travels across to reach us. . . ."

I stopped. "Guys?"

Mike and Lisa were over at the fence, ignoring me.

"Come on back," I said.

"I like it when you talk about God," Mike said. "But enough of the science."

"I'm done," I promised.

A shooting star flashed across the night sky.

Meteor, I thought. Burning from the friction of its speed through the atmosphere.

I shook my head and mentally corrected myself with a smile. The shooting star was a nice present from God, I thought. Even if I had bored my friends to death, at least *He* was listening to me.

"Do we tell your parents now about the statue?" Lisa asked a few minutes later. "After all, if this white-haired guy is entering Norbert's house, he could be dangerous. And I'm sure it has something to do with the statue. He tried taking it from me this afternoon at the beach."

"I just don't get it," I said. "You saw Norbert in the white-haired guy's car. It's like he's in on this. But why would he want the guy to steal a scarf from his fiancée? And for that matter, why hasn't Norbert come back? He doesn't know that we know he's involved. From his point of view, he has nothing to be afraid of."

"He's afraid of getting married," Mike said. "You heard Anna talk about it."

"And I also heard Anna talk about his bad invest-ments," Lisa said. "I think that's what's behind this. It really seemed like he's crazy about her. I think he would marry her except for whatever is happening with this statue."

There was a kissing sound. Mike had put the back of his hand to his lips and smacked loudly. "Yes," he said in a theatrical voice. "True love."

He kissed the back of his hand again.

"Men," Lisa said.

"I certainly don't think that's funny, Mike," I said in a disapproving voice. Actually, I did think it was funny, but there was no sense in Lisa being mad at both of us.

"So . . ." Lisa said.

"So?" I echoed. Sometimes girls switch subjects, and when they do, other girls know exactly what subject is the new one, but guys are almost always in the dark.

"So do we tell your parents and Anna about the statue?"

Oh, that was the subject.

"Remember," I answered, "they agreed they couldn't report Norbert as missing because forty-eight hours haven't passed. And they hope and believe he'll still show up. To me, that says enough."

"To me," Lisa said, "you're not making sense."

"If Norbert shows up, he can explain everything. And who knows, there might be a very reasonable explanation for this."

Mike snorted. "Right."

"Come on," I said. "We should give him the benefit of the doubt. If we go to my parents with a bunch of suspicious things that don't make sense, it's unfairly making Norbert look bad. You know, innocent until proven guilty."

"You don't think he looks bad enough by now?" Lisa countered. "He left to get cream for coffee ten hours ago.

And hasn't made it back. Without even a phone call to tell his best friend from college and a houseful of guests and his fiancée where he's gone."

"Forty-eight hours," I said, thinking of how my dad would be disappointed to hear any accusations against his best friend. "If he's not back by then, we'll go to my parents."

"Fine with me," Mike said. "After all, what can go wrong in the next thirty-eight hours?"

As it turned out, plenty.

And it started just a few hours later, with me waking up in the dark in the middle of the night with a gloved hand covering my mouth so that I couldn't yell for help.

CHAPTER 16

"Mmmmpppph." That muffled noise was all that I could force out. "Mmmmmmmpph."

Thirty seconds earlier I'd been sound asleep and dreaming. My subconscious must have picked up the fact that someone had entered the bedroom, because in my dream I'd been in a small room with a beeping robot about to attack me. I'd opened my eyes to the faint smell of men's aftershave lotion as a man leaned over me, and before I could even sit up, the gloved hand had clamped itself against my mouth.

"Mmmmmmmph."

"Where is it?" It was a whisper. "I know you've got it with you. Where is it? Under the pillow?"

"Mmmmmmmph." How could I answer with the hand on my mouth?

The man's other hand reached under my pillow. I knew he wouldn't find the statue. I'd put it under the mattress after Mike and Lisa voted for me to keep it safe. My entire body weight was keeping it safe.

"Mmmmmmph." I wanted to scream. Mike and Lisa were in different bedrooms just down the hallway. Mom and Dad were nearby in another bedroom. All of that help so close by, but there was nothing they could do if they didn't know what was happening here.

"Where is it!" The whisper seemed loud and harsh.

"Mmmmph."

The hand pressed harder against my face. Now I could hardly breath.

"I'm going to let go, and I want you to tell me very quietly where it is." His face was right up against my ear. "I really don't want to hurt you, but you don't want to find out what will happen if I hear you suck in a deep breath to scream."

He began to lift his hand.

Just down the hall, Rachel began to cry for another bottle. Four times a night this happened. She'd wake up hungry and let the whole world know it. Usually it made me grumpy when she woke the entire house. Now I was glad. Mom or Dad would get up.

Then sudden fear filled me like a fire. If Mom or Dad saw this guy, he would attack without warning. And if it was Mom getting the bottle, she might be seriously hurt.

Dear God, I prayed silently, *please keep this man from hurting them.*

I held my breath as a door somewhere in the house opened. A light clicked on in the kitchen.

"It's okay, little one," Mom called out to Rachel.

I closed my eyes against my fear. I hoped Mom

wouldn't notice anything wrong in my room. I didn't want her hurt.

The man pressed his face closer to mine. "I'm going to go. Remember, I really don't want to hurt you. But if you say a word about this to anyone, I'll find a way to make you miserable. Understand? You keep this quiet. Nod, and I'll let go. But if you yell, I'll have to fight my way out of this house. And that won't be good."

I nodded. Quickly. There was no way I was going to put Mom in danger.

And just like that, the pressure was off my face.

The man vanished from my bedroom.

I held my breath longer.

What if Mom ran into him as he was escaping the house?

Rachel's crying suddenly stopped. I let out my breath. I knew Mom had brought her a bottle and was holding Rachel as she fed her.

They were safe. I dropped my head back on the pillow and in the darkness blinked away tears of anger and fear.

I didn't sleep for the rest of the night.

Two questions kept coming back to haunt me again and again and again.

How had this guy gotten into the house?

And how had he known that the statue was in my room and somewhere in my bed?

CHAPTER  17

"One hundred and thirty thousand gallons of molten lava every minute!" Mike whistled as he leafed through the guidebook. "Cool."

"Actually," Dad said, "hot."

Dad looked around the deck and waited for the rest of us to laugh at his joke. Since Mom was getting Rachel ready to join us on our day trip across the island, the rest of us meant Mike and Lisa and Joel and me, leaning back in our chairs in the mid-morning sunshine.

Dad cleared his throat. "Let me point out that I rented the van, I'll be driving all of you across the island, and I'll be taking care of buying gasoline, lunch, and any admission passes to Hawaii Volcanoes National Park."

"I get it!" I said. "Mike thinks it will be cool to see all that flowing lava, but you meant lava has to be hot to flow." I faked laughter.

So did Mike and Lisa.

"That's better." Dad grinned. "Let me see if you

learned your lesson. Why did the chicken cross the road?"

He paused. "To get to the other side."

Mike slapped his knees as he laughed. I held my stomach as if it hurt to laugh. Lisa snorted through her nose.

Sitting beside Dad, Joel just stared at us.

"Fast learners, aren't you?" Dad said. He ruffled Joel's hair. "Except for you."

"Why did it want to get to the other side?" Joel asked. "It might get run over."

He didn't like the thought of animals getting hurt.

"I'll explain it to you on the way there," I told Joel.

"And I'll keep explaining Hawaii Volcanoes National Park," Mike said.

"Please don't," Lisa told him. "We've all read the guidebook already."

Mike ignored her and held the guidebook just below his chest as he read. "The present eruption began in 1983. It produces a river of moving lava that is capable of sensing the cooler temperatures of nearby human beings. As if drawn by a magnet to the cooler temperatures, the lava will shift direction quickly to devour unwary humans, or those too slow to outrun the average horse. The lava then quickly melts all human flesh and leaves behind fossilized bones. Entire families have been found preserved this way, yet are occasionally mistaken for clusters of dinosaur bones. Therefore—"

Lisa jerked the guidebook away from him. "Nice try. All you had correct was the date of the current eruption. The slow-moving lava presents no threat to visitors."

"But I bet it would melt their flesh," Mike said. "And fossilize their—"

"Mike!" Lisa sighed. "Is this the kind of stuff you want Joel to put in his school reports? Maturity is a virtue, you know."

"Actually," he said. "I *didn't* know that. I—"

This time it wasn't Lisa who interrupted him.

But Joseph Norbert. Stepping onto the deck from the inside of his beach house.

We all froze with surprise.

"Hello," he said. "I'll bet you wondered where I went yesterday and last night."

He smiled. "It's a long story and pretty funny, and I'll tell you on my wedding day. Can you wait until then?"

We all nodded. What choice did we have? We were his guests.

"Well," he continued, breaking the awkward silence. "I hear you're all going to the volcano park. I'd love to come along."

Norbert spoke to Dad. "Got room in the rental van?"

"You bet," Dad replied.

"I noticed it's locked and you've already got your gear in there. Any chance I can borrow the keys for a second? I want to throw a couple of things in myself."

Dad threw him the keys. "We're almost ready to go."

"Back in two minutes," Norbert said.

I stood quickly. "Let me come with you. I need something out of the van."

Norbert frowned, as if he didn't want me to go with him. But I smiled politely, and that didn't give Norbert much choice. I wasn't going to let him go alone. Because Lisa's gym bag was in the van. With the statue hidden inside.

I think somehow he knew that. And I believed he wanted to steal it while we were waiting for Mom and Rachel.

How did I know all of this?

Simple.

The slight breeze across the deck had brought me the smell of his aftershave.

The same aftershave I'd smelled in the darkness barely hours earlier. When someone had pressed a gloved hand onto my mouth and demanded the statue I'd hidden under my mattress.

CHAPTER 18

I had no chance to tell Mike or Lisa this. Less than a minute later Mom showed up with Rachel. Dad loaded Rachel into a car seat, and all of us piled in. With Norbert in the van beside us, I had to simply join in all the small talk.

The drive itself was very interesting. Mike kept swinging his video camera out the window to catch the changing scenery.

We left from the west side—the Kona side. West Hawaii had almost been a shock to us upon arrival. It was hot and dry and always sunny, with black lava covering much of the land and beaches made of salt-and-pepper sand. But only fifteen minutes inland were the coffee plantation mountains—lush and green and cool and quiet.

From the west side, the only road to take across the island first went south, bringing us to the southern tip of the island, which was also the most southern point in the United States. Then we headed east and then northeast, which took us through the Kau Desert. We could see the rise of

Mauna Loa, Hawaii's thirteen-thousand-foot-high mountain, part of the Hawaii Volcanoes National Park. The top
of the mountain was shrouded in mist. Although I felt nervous around Norbert and questions about him swirled
through my mind, I was still able to imagine what it might
be like at the summit of that mountain, high enough to
hold snow.

As we crossed the desert, Norbert explained the reason
for it. As air rose up the mountains on the east side of
Hawaii, it dropped all its moisture. When it fell down the
opposite side, into the desert, it was dry. Norbert told us
that the east side was the exact opposite of the west side
of the island. Cool. Wet. Rain forests and tropical flowers.

As I listened to him, I kept trying to figure things out.

If it really was him the night before in my room, I now
understood why he'd been able to break into the house so
easily.

But why?

To get the statue.

Except how did he know I'd had it hidden under my
mattress? And if he'd wanted to get into the van because
of it, how had he known it was there this morning?

Why, when he'd seen Joel with the statue, hadn't he
reacted? Was it because he didn't want us to know that he
knew about it?

Who was the white-haired guy with earrings? If, as
Lisa said, Norbert had been in the car with him at the
beach, then Norbert and the white-haired guy were working together. But if they were working together, why had
the white-haired guy stepped in Norbert's house the day

before simply to steal a white scarf from Anna while she was sleeping?

And why had Norbert disappeared for nearly twenty-four hours, only to show up like nothing had ever happened?

I thought about the Dumpster, the fishing buoy, Norbert knocking Mike overboard as I was reeling in the shark.

None of it fit together. None of it—

"Richard!" My mom's voice broke through my thoughts. "We're here."

So we were.

As Lisa opened the doors, sulfur fumes hit my nose.

A cloud passed in front of the sun, and the moist green vegetation in all directions seemed ominous.

Especially with Norbert getting out of the van behind me.

"We've got a walkie-talkie," Lisa told my mom and dad. "You've got another one. We won't be going far, so we can stay in touch. Sound good?"

Dad finally nodded.

We stood at the base of a trail. The parking lot, full of vehicles, was behind us. Mike and Lisa and I had asked for permission to go ahead by ourselves. Something about tagging along with a six-year-old and a baby in a stroller and three adults didn't quite seem to be the perfect Hawaii moment.

"Remember," Lisa said, "keep it on channel 10."

In her right hand, Lisa carried her gym bag. It had sandwiches and water and, of course, the statue. While Mom and Dad had gone to pay for the park pass, I'd been able to explain to Lisa and Mike about Norbert's midnight visit the night before. We weren't about to leave the statue behind for him to take at his leisure.

"Channel 10," Mom repeated. "Got it."

"Don't worry," I said. "It's not like we'll start swimming in lava or anything like that."

Of course, I wasn't counting on someone planning to throw us into the molten river.

We followed a path upward through the thick vegetation. We'd been walking for about half an hour. It seemed like we were entirely alone in this weird, new world, with mists and sulfur smells and strange birdcalls and thick ferns and bright flowers.

According to the map, we could expect to see a lava flow from the top of the next rise.

"Hey," Mike said. "Listen."

Lisa and I stopped.

"Birds," I said.

"More than that. I heard beeping."

"Sure, Mike," I said. "Beeping."

"Shhh!" Lisa said. "I heard it, too."

"Birdcalls," I insisted. I was behind both of them. I took a step forward and pushed Mike so that he would continue. Then I stopped again. Not to listen for more beeping. But because of an unfamiliar voice directly behind us.

"You've gone far enough," the voice said.

The white-haired guy with earrings stepped out from behind a fern. He grinned at us, and it seemed all the more creepy because of the mirror reflection in his wraparound sunglasses.

In one hand was a small knapsack. In the other was a black object that looked like a wide wand.

"I'll take the gym bag," he continued. He placed the black wand into his knapsack and pulled out a roll of gray duct tape. "And this time you don't have any choice."

"Run!" I shouted to Lisa. "We'll find tourists over the next hill."

All three of us burst forward. The white-haired guy crashed through ferns as he began to give chase.

We crested the hill and saw the glowing orange lava cutting a path beside the lush green vegetation. But we saw no other tourists. The path took us downward and then up again.

And that's where he managed to dive forward and catch me by the ankle. I fell face forward, stunned. In less than two seconds he'd wrapped my wrists together.

"Stop," he shouted to Mike and Lisa. He wrapped my ankles with duct tape. "Turn around and come back. Unless you want me to barbecue your friend in this nearby lava."

CHAPTER 19

"Here's the way it's going to work," the white-haired guy said. He had already taken the statue from Lisa's gym bag and placed it inside his knapsack.

Mike and I were on the ground, hands and feet taped. Lisa sat beside us. Her hands and feet were taped, too. She glared at the white-haired guy.

I kept hoping for other tourists to come over the crest and find us. But it was unlikely. He'd dragged us off the path, toward the lava. The vegetation was so thick, we had disappeared from the sight of the path almost immediately.

"Are you working with Norbert?" I asked.

"The less you know the better," he answered. "Really. That's how it is for me, too. I don't know who gets this statue, and I don't want to know."

He pulled a knife from the bag.

I tried to hide my fear. This was not good.

Then the voices of tourists!

I opened my mouth to yell, but he spoke quickly.

"No noise, or I roll you into the lava. You'll be long dead and I'll be long gone before those people find you among all these ferns."

I made no noise. Neither did Lisa or Mike. The lava was close enough we could feel warmth in the air. The sulfur smell was almost overpowering. Maybe those two, like me, were thinking about how Mike had joked about melting flesh and fossilized bones.

"That's smart," the white-haired guy said with approval. "Because I don't want to hurt you. I got what I wanted, and that should be enough."

He smiled and pulled out his roll of duct tape again. "But it won't hurt to have insurance."

He slapped a piece of tape over my mouth, then Mike's, then Lisa's. My eyes bugged as I watched him wave the knife at us.

"You see, all I need is a five-minute head start." He set the knife just beyond us on a flat rock. "I'm going to leave this for you. With teamwork, one of you will be able to pick it up and cut through the tape of someone else. In less than ten minutes you'll all be free. Then go ahead and continue sight-seeing. You won't be able to find me by then anyway, and no harm's been done to you. Let this rest."

He spoke earnestly. "Listen. The statue wasn't yours in the first place, and it's never been any of your business. Whoever owns it will get it now, and life will continue as if nothing ever happened. If you went to the police with your story, you'd have no evidence. And if you went to the police, I would probably be sent to punish you guys. Remember how easily I was able to take Anna's scarf. That was to prove to Norbert that—"

He cut himself short and shook his head. "Let's just say I don't want to hurt you. Just like I didn't want to hurt Anna. So please, don't tell anybody about this. Not your parents. Not the police. And I won't have to show up some-day and hurt you."

He shrugged. "That's all I have to say. Good-bye."

With that, he stepped into the deep green vegetation and disappeared.

With the statue.

CHAPTER  20

We didn't get home until eight o'clock that night. Too late to have a live chat with Ralphy. But he'd sent an e-mail. I read it out loud to Mike and Lisa from my computer screen.

—— Original Message ——
From: "Ralphy Zee" *zeer@coolmail.com*
To: "Ricky Kidd" *kiddr@coolmail.com*
Subject: No April Fool's This Time!

Guys,

The Internet is great! What I did was send some e-mail inquiries with the JPEG of the picture of the statue to directors at different museums around the world. I finally heard back from someone in Los Angeles. It turns out that my April Fool's joke wasn't that much of a joke. The statue really is worth millions!

This is where it gets weirder.

The director of that Los Angeles museum says that it is a famous antique statue that belongs to a Tokyo museum. So I sent an e-mail inquiry there, expecting someone to tell me it had been stolen.

But it hasn't! Do you guys have a fake? Or is there a fake in the museum in Tokyo?

What next? I don't know. But the Los Angeles director also sent me a list of different Japanese artwork experts to talk to if I ever had any more questions.

And guess what . . .

One of the foremost experts in the world is a private collector of Japanese artwork who lives . . .

(drum roll please)

. . . on the west side of the big island of Hawaii. Close to you guys! His name is Trenton Matrick. Maybe you could ask him to look at the statue and tell you if it is fake or real.

Ralphy

"Hah, hah," Mike said when I finished reading the e-mail to them. "Pretty tough to ask this Matrick guy to look at the statue when we don't have it anymore."

"Norbert's probably got it," I said.

"Doesn't make sense," Lisa said. "If Norbert wanted it, why would he send the white-haired guy after us? Why not just wait for a good chance to take it?"

"Especially because it seems both of them knew exactly where it was," Mike said. "First the white-haired guy trying to take Lisa's bag on the beach. Then Norbert going into Ricky's bedroom last night. Then the white-haired guy managing to find us in the volcano park. It's like they can locate it whenever they want."

It's like they can locate it whenever they want.

"Maybe," I said quietly, "because they can."

On the computer, I shut down my e-mail program. My fingers clicked on keys as I continued to speak. "Remember we decided if Norbert and the white-haired guy were working together, maybe Norbert told the white-haired guy about Lisa and sat in the car at the beach."

I opened a video display program on my laptop. My hard drive whirred as it loaded. "And we thought maybe it was a lucky guess that Norbert went into my bedroom. But the thing is, even if the white-haired guy knew we were going to the volcano park, it would have been impossible to track us. And would he really have driven hours to follow our van across the island on just the possibility we had the statue with us?"

I leaned back and pointed to my computer screen.

"My video footage of the white-haired guy at the marina," Mike said. "What does that have to do with—"

"Mike!" This came from Lisa. "Look at what he's doing on the boat."

We had already seen this once before, of course. Just after Mike had been in the Dumpster. It was about four minutes of video. It showed the marina with the different-sized sailboats. It showed the white-haired guy on Norbert's boat. It wasn't a close-up, though; Mike had had to shoot it from a boat far enough away to stay hidden from the guy.

"He's leaning over the buoys," Mike said. "I was there, remember?"

My fingers clicked again. I froze the video and zoomed in.

"Now look," I said to Mike. "See what Lisa's talking about?"

He frowned, puzzled. "Yeah. It's the same kind of wand

thing he had in the volcano park."

Exactly. That's why I'd brought up the program. After hearing Mike say it was as if they could locate the statue any time, it jogged my memory.

"Looks like a global positioning system," I said. "Like the one that Norbert had on his—"

I stopped myself.

Like the one that Norbert had on his boat.

I smacked my forehead. "I am so dumb," I moaned.

"Often," Mike said, grinning. "What is it this time?"

On Norbert's boat. When I'd been close to catching the shark. All the beeping that kept getting louder and louder. His GPS. It had been locating something all right.

A fishing buoy. But one that didn't belong to him.

"We've had it wrong from the beginning," I said. "Norbert wasn't trying to deliver the statue. He went shark fishing that morning to pick it up."

I explained how it made sense. Norbert didn't want to take us that morning, but Dad insisted until Norbert couldn't think of a reasonable excuse to say no. He took us out into the darkness, probably expecting that he could locate the fishing buoy and pretend he'd found it by accident. After all, we wouldn't know what was inside it. Unfortunately, I'd hooked the shark at about the same time it was floating past us. So Norbert cut my line and pushed Mike overboard as a way to distract us. Then he pretended he was looking for the missing buoy, but he was actually looking for another one, the one he was supposed to pick up.

I finished.

Mike nodded slowly.

"Ricky," he said, "remember there was a fishing trawler that floated past us that morning. You asked Norbert if it might hit us in the dark."

My turn to nod.

"What if someone dropped it from the trawler?" Mike asked.

"And what if it was a Japanese fishing trawler?" Lisa added. "With someone on the boat delivering a statue to Hawaii?"

"Well," I said, "there are two ways to find out. And the simplest way is to tell Norbert what we know and ask him to give us the truth."

"No," Lisa said. "We go to your mom and dad. The statue might be worth millions. It's time to involve them."

"*Might* be worth millions," Mike told her. "It could be a fake. Not only that, but we don't even have it. I don't think Norbert would admit anything. And we have no proof. I think that leaves the second way. Whatever it is."

They looked at me, waiting.

"Which is to fight fire with fire," I said. "Tomorrow we're going to rent some mountain bikes and see if we can't get the statue back."

"How are we going to find it?" Mike asked.

I grinned. And told them.

CHAPTER 21

"Wow," Mike said. "This Matrick guy must have a lot of money."

With our rented mountain bikes leaning against our hips, we stood in front of a wide gate at the beginning of a long driveway. We'd found Trenton Matrick's address in the phone book, and it had been a short bike ride to there from Norbert's beach house.

We saw easily through the gaps between the iron bars of the gate. They showed a lush green lawn dotted with palm trees and layered everywhere with beautiful flower beds. Up at the mansion, a Jaguar was parked in front of a four-car garage.

"Now what?" Mike asked. The entire property was surrounded by a ten-foot-high brick wall. This gate was the only way in. "Climb over?"

"I think we ring the bell on the wall here and smile into the video camera," I told Mike. I pointed at it, perched on top of the brick wall. "Then we tell whoever answers why we are here."

"Climbing is more fun," he said.

"Running away from Dobermans is not."

"Huh?"

I pointed at a distant flower garden. Just beyond it, two massive guard dogs were trotting toward us.

"Smart man," he said. "Maybe I'll just ring the bell."

"You have three minutes to explain this nonsense about a Japanese warrior statue." Trenton Matrick stood in the front hallway of his mansion. He loomed over us. "I don't like wasting time with children and foolish nonsense."

I wanted to tell him that nonsense was foolish and that he was being repetitive. But it didn't seem like a good idea. Not with the frown on his face.

Trenton Matrick wore black pants and a black silk shirt. He had thinning gray hair and was probably in his fifties or sixties. He wore thick gold rings, a watch with a gold face, and a heavy gold chain.

"Out with it," he said. "At the gate you mentioned something about a Japanese warrior statue."

Which was true. Mike had rung the bell. A man's voice had informed us he had no interest in magazine subscriptions, school fund-raisers, or giving directions to lost children. When I'd said we knew something about a missing Japanese warrior statue, he'd told us to wait while he called his dogs in. Then the gate had swung open and Mike and

I had pedaled up the driveway.

"Yes, sir," I said. "We know you're an expert on Japanese artwork. We found this statue a few days ago, and we wondered if you could help us locate the owner."

From my back pocket I pulled out a folded piece of paper. Just after breakfast I'd used a printer at Norbert's house and printed off the digital scan of the Japanese warrior. Norbert hadn't been around for me to ask permission, but I didn't think he would have minded.

I opened the paper and held it out. Trenton grabbed it from my hand.

"You found this? Where?"

"In a Dumpster," I said. "My friend here . . ." I pointed at Mike.

Mike groaned. "I feel awful. I think I had too many pancakes." He gagged and clapped a hand over his mouth. "The bathroom. I think I'm going to . . ."

"Down the hall!" Trenton commanded. "On your right. If you make a mess, I'll set my dogs on you!"

Mike ran. The floor was marble, the walls were dark walnut, and expensive artwork hung everywhere.

"Continue," Trenton commanded me in the same tone of voice. "You found it in a Dumpster. . . ."

I told him most of the story. That after we found it, some white-haired guy had tried taking it from us at the beach, then had stolen it from us at the volcano park.

"So maybe it's valuable," I finished. "It's like this guy really wanted it bad. But we don't know much about the statue, and we don't know if we should go to the police."

Trenton stared at me thoughtfully. He studied the

paper more carefully. Finally he declared judgment on the statue.

"My guess is that it's junk," he said. "I'd have to actually see it and hold it to be sure, but if you found it in a Dumpster—and I don't even want to guess why you'd gone there in the first place—obviously someone threw it out. Probably someone who hadn't even been able to get rid of it at a yard sale. I think if you go to the police, they'll laugh you out of the station."

"I see," I said. "But this white-haired guy seemed to want it bad. And we don't even know who he is. It's like..."

I paused. I needed to stall as long as possible. "...it's like he was crazy about the statue."

"Then it was probably something he won in a bowling league, and his wife hated it and threw it out. Really, I don't have time for any more of this foolish nonsense of yours."

Maybe foolish nonsense was a favorite phrase. I really wanted to point out how unneeded it was to keep describing nonsense as foolish.

"Bowling league, sir? Do you bowl?"

His face began to turn red. "Enough. Now get your friend and—"

"Mr. Matrick?" A large, large man with a short, short brush cut stepped into the hallway. He held Mike by the collar of his shirt.

"Sorry, Ricky," Mike said. His voice was high-pitched and strangled. His feet dangled high off the ground. "I couldn't manage to wrestle this guy to the ground."

"Watch what you're doing with that boy," Trenton said to the large man. "If he throws up . . ."

"I don't think he is sick, sir. I found him wandering around with this."

The large man—probably a bodyguard—held out his other hand. He showed Trenton Matrick a flat black wand. Like the one the white-haired guy had used to locate us in the volcano park.

We had found this wand on Norbert's boat.

"A locator?" Matrick thundered. "What was he doing with a locator?"

"It appeared he was looking for your statue. I found him with it in the study."

"I see," Matrick said much more quietly. He grabbed my wrist and pulled me toward the bodyguard. "We'll lock them up in the pool house with the other two. I guess tonight the sharks are really going to have a feast."

CHAPTER 22

They dragged Mike and me through the mansion and outside to the pool area. Beyond the pool was a small white building in the shade beneath a palm tree.

"That's the pool house?" I asked. "The white building? Can't you keep us anywhere else? I don't like small spaces."

"And I don't like snoopy juveniles," Matrick said. He was surprisingly strong for an older man. "When you're swimming with the sharks tonight, you'll wish you were still in the pool house."

"We told my parents we were coming here," I said. "You'll get caught. Killing us will put you in prison for a—"

"You'll be long gone before the police get a warrant to search here," Matrick answered. "Rest assured, they won't find any traces of your visit. I'm not too worried about getting caught."

I had plenty of other questions for Matrick, but I didn't want him to realize how much Mike and I knew. I'd already said what I needed to, and I could only hope our plan wouldn't fall apart now. So I remained silent for the rest of the short walk to the pool house.

Duct tape seemed to be in fashion as a way to tie up kids, because that's what they used on our wrists and ankles.

"Don't even think about trying to leave before tonight," Matrick said. "My guard dogs will be camped outside, waiting for the chance to take a few chunks out of you before the sharks get their fill."

He seemed to enjoy telling this to us. Once again I hoped our plan would work.

"Please," I said. "Let me ask you one last time. Don't do this."

"Hah," Matrick snorted. "I've spent far too many years and far too much money building up my collection to let a couple of brats get in the way."

Without ceremony, he opened the door to the pool house. The bodyguard rolled me inside. Then Mike.

The door shut behind us, and the lock clicked shut.

There were no windows to let us escape. The sunlight poured through a skylight. Robes hung neatly from hooks. The inside smelled of chlorine and of freshly laundered towels.

It also smelled of the same aftershave I'd smelled when

someone had pressed my head down on my pillow in the middle of the night.

There was a good reason for that smell.

Joseph Norbert was already in the pool house, leaning against one wall with his wrists and ankles also wrapped tightly in duct tape.

Just like the other person sharing our prison. The white-haired, muscled guy with earrings.

"Dude," Mike said with a big grin to the white-haired guy. "Nice to see you again."

CHAPTER 23

"My friends call me Jimmy," the white-haired guy said. "You might as well do the same."

"Friends?" I'd been able to squirm into a sitting position beside Mike. "You attacked Lisa on the beach. Then you threatened to barbecue us in lava."

"Yeah," Mike said. "That doesn't sound friendly to me."

"Jimmy was doing his best to save you guys from Matrick." Norbert sighed. He pulled his knees up in front of him and shifted a few times to make himself more comfortable. "As for me, I should have sent your whole family back to Jamesville as soon as this started going wrong. But I thought . . ."

"Hey," Jimmy said. "Neither of us saw this happening. What I'd really like to know is how you guys got the statue in the first place."

Mike explained.

Then I explained my guess about the global positioning locator.

"You both worked for Matrick?" I asked. "He

sent you out to get the statue, right?"

"Yes and no," Jimmy said. "I mean, I worked for him and he was the one who sent me out, but I didn't know it was him. About a year ago, while I was lifting weights in the gym, some guy—now I know it was his bodyguard—left an envelope beside me with a note saying all I had to do was follow instructions from someone over the telephone. I needed the money. I was behind on loan payments. My job was to take a fishing buoy off Norbert's boat and leave it in a Dumpster. That was it. Matrick went to a lot of work to protect himself."

"Protect himself?" Mike echoed.

"Sure. It was a system with two links. Norbert didn't know it was me who picked stuff up from his boat after he went shark fishing. And I didn't know who would take it out of the Dumpster after I left it there."

"So we were right," I said to Norbert. "You went out shark fishing to pick stuff up."

"I'd lost a lot of money in stock trading," Norbert said. "I was so behind on mortgage payments that I was about to lose my house. Then I got a letter one day. All I knew was I had to go out there to collect a fishing buoy at a specific time and location about once every month. For that, I received twenty thousand dollars in cash, left under my boat seat at noon each of the days I went out and returned."

He closed his eyes and looked down. "I just wish you and Mike would have a chance to learn from my mistake. Give in to a little temptation, and it leads to a bigger one. And that leads to a bigger one and bigger one, until, without knowing it, you're in way over your head and there's no way to get out."

He lifted his eyes again. I noticed they were filled with tears. "I went from just making trips to pick something up to betraying my best friend from college and lying to the woman I loved."

He lapsed into silence.

"See," Jimmy said, "when Matrick found the buoy empty—"

"He went into the garbage after the truck emptied the Dumpster?" Mike asked.

"Dude, he *owns* the garbage."

"Huh?"

"That's what made him his fortune. He runs landfills. It was the perfect system. He knew what truck would pick up the garbage from the Dumpster. At night he'd send his bodyguard in with a locator to retrieve it. That way he could claim he'd found the statue and all his other collectibles in the garbage. Which was true. What he wouldn't tell if he was caught was that there were fakes in place for all the pieces he'd collected from museums around the world."

"He told you all this," I said.

Jimmy shrugged. "He knows we're going to die. It's like he wanted to brag to someone about his system. Even about the part where he found a couple of desperate guys by paying a banker friend to give him the names of anyone who was really behind on loan payments."

"So when Matrick found the fishing buoy empty a couple of days ago..." I prompted.

"I got a visit from the bodyguard the next morning. Only I still didn't know it was Matrick sending the bodyguard. The guy threatened to kill me if I didn't give him the statue. I told him that Norbert must have emptied it. That's when I called Norbert."

"During breakfast," Norbert said quietly. "That's why I had to sneak away. Jimmy told me over the telephone he'd find a way to hurt my fiancée if I didn't help him recover it. He even stole a scarf from her while she was sleeping. That's when I knew he could do it."

"You went to the beach with Jimmy and pointed us out," Mike said.

Norbert nodded. "That didn't work. That night I tried taking it from my own house. I had the locator. And that didn't work, either. The next morning I called Jimmy on his cell and told him it was in the gym bag. He followed the rental van to the volcano park and took it from you there. I thought I was safe."

"Boy, were we wrong," Jimmy said. "All along Matrick planned to get rid of us once we got the statue back to him. He figured it was too dangerous, with us knowing more about his operation than he wanted. This morning when I delivered the statue, his bodyguard pulled a gun on me."

"And I got another phone call," Norbert said, "promising me money. I showed up here and the same thing happened to me."

Norbert strained to pull his wrists apart. The muscles in his neck bulged, his face turned red, and veins looked like snakes in his massive arms. But the tape didn't rip.

"So that's it," he said, puffing. "We sit here until dark.

Then they roll us onto a truck, onto a boat, and out into the water."

"Maybe not," I said. "I think in about five minutes the police will arrive."

"What!" Norbert's eyes opened wide with sudden hope.

"Under my shorts, I taped a walkie-talkie to my leg," I said. "With the call button wide open. Lisa's just down the road at a pay phone. From her walkie-talkie, she's taped everything into a cassette recorder from the moment Mike and I walked up Matrick's driveway."

I paused. "Right, Lisa? You can come in now. I think we have enough."

The next second was the longest of my life.

Finally she answered.

"Right, Ricky." Her voice was fuzzy, coming from the walkie-talkie Mike had taped to his leg underneath his shorts. "I've already called the police from this pay phone. They are on their way."

EPILOGUE

The next Saturday Joseph Norbert stood at the front of the church in a black tuxedo. Anna stood beside him, beautiful in her white dress.

"I now pronounce you man and wife," a tall minister with gray hair and a deep voice said to both of them. "You may now kiss the bride."

Norbert leaned toward Anna and lifted her veil.

"Eww." Mike turned his head sideways and grimaced. Lisa elbowed him.

As for me, I turned my eyes back toward Joel. He sat beside me, with Mike and Lisa on the other side of him. Mom and Rachel were two pews in front of us. Dad, as best man, was standing near the groom. The small church was filled with friends of Norbert and Anna.

"Joel," I hissed. I'd seen strange movements in the sleeve of his coat, and I was getting more and more nervous. Joel had never been shy about making friends with various animals and taking them into public places.

The minister turned to all of us and spoke

gravely. "May I now introduce Joseph and Anna Norbert."

The congregation stood, and organ music swelled and filled the church.

Joseph and Anna began a slow, dignified walk down the aisle.

Anna looked very happy, even though her new husband was out on bail and would be in court in a month or two. Norbert's lawyers said he might have to do some probationary time, but that was probably the maximum. Indirectly, thanks to Norbert, Trenton Matrick had been caught as a collector of millions of dollars worth of stolen museum pieces from around the world. With Norbert's testimony, Matrick was the one who would face a long time in prison, for theft and attempted murder.

"Richard!" Lisa tugged on my shoulder. "Pay attention."

I had been paying attention. But not to the wedding. I kept my eyes on Joel's sleeve.

And in that moment I was rewarded.

I saw the head of a garter snake peek out of his sleeve.

"Hah," I said.

I reached down and grabbed Joel's wrist, trapping the snake. It felt like a thin piece of rope beneath his jacket sleeve.

"Don't move," I said to Joel. Slowly, very slowly, I reached up his sleeve with my free hand. I got a grip on the snake just behind its head. The last thing I wanted to see was that snake getting loose in the church.

Just as I had the snake halfway out of Joel's sleeve, Norbert and Anna passed by us in the aisle. With my right hand, I held tight to the snake, terrified it would choose this moment to dart loose.

I jammed it into my pants pocket and kept my hand there. It was a tiny snake, and it wriggled in a ball around my fingers.

The music continued to play.

Row by row, people began to empty out of the pews.

Norbert and Anna stood by the doorway, accepting congratulations from everyone who passed through.

"This is taking forever," Mike groaned. "I'll starve to death before we get to the wedding buffet."

I agreed. This did seem like it was taking forever. I had a small snake in my right-hand pocket. And I had a younger brother glaring at me for being a bully and taking it away from him. I could hardly wait to get out of the church to let the snake go.

We finally reached the entrance. I tried to squeeze past Norbert and Anna.

She reached for me and hugged me. With my left arm, I hugged her back. I carefully kept my right hand in my pocket.

"Thank you," she whispered. She kissed my cheek and let me go.

I sighed with relief. Only a few more steps and I could get rid of the snake.

"Not so fast," Norbert said to me above the organ music. "I owe you a lot. Not only did I learn my lesson, but it looks like I'll have a chance to put my life back together."

"Yes, sir," I said. "That's great."

Dad and Mom and Rachel were somewhere behind me. Ahead was freedom.

Norbert stuck out his hand to shake mine. "Thanks," he said.

I kept my right hand in my pocket.

"Come on," Norbert said. "No hard feelings."

"None," I said, a smile frozen on my face.

"Then shake on it," he said.

I hesitated.

"Come on," Mike said to me, "you're holding up the line and I'm starving."

I hesitated more. A hurt look crossed Norbert's face.

Before I could explain, Mike repeated himself. "Come on, Ricky. Shake hands. He just got married."

Mike jerked on my arm, pulling my hand out of my pocket.

And there it was. For Norbert and Anna and the entire church to see. A green, wriggling snake intertwined in my fingers.

A woman beside me screamed. Then another. And a whole stampede of them headed to the door.

I hung my head.

"Good one, Ricky," Mike said as the confusion worsened. "What did you have planned for the banquet? A jar of cockroaches?"

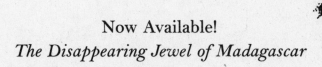

Now Available!
The Disappearing Jewel of Madagascar

Friends become strangers, and strangers become friends. . . .

When Ricky Kidd first hears about the curse of the Jewel of Madagascar, he is pretty sure he doesn't believe in it. But almost immediately, strange things start happening. First he knocks over a statue that crushes part of Mrs. McEwan's antique jewelry collection. Ricky is convinced his life is over—paying off the debt will take years!

As if that weren't bad enough, all of his friends seem to be deliberately avoiding him. And then there is Mrs. McEwan's mysterious nephew— Ricky is sure he is not who he seems. Can the curse be coming true? As Ricky struggles to make sense of everything, he learns the importance of friends, trust, and loyalty.

Series for Middle Graders* From BHP

THE ACCIDENTAL DETECTIVES · by Sigmund Brouwer
Action-packed adventures lead Ricky Kidd and his friends into places they never dreamed of, drawing them closer with every step.

ADVENTURES DOWN UNDER · by Robert Elmer
When Patrick McWaid's father is unjustly sent to Australia as a prisoner in 1867, the rest of the family follows, uncovering action-packed mystery along the way.

ADVENTURES OF THE NORTHWOODS · by Lois Walfrid Johnson
Kate O'Connell and her stepbrother Anders encounter mystery and adventure in northwest Wisconsin near the turn of the century.

BLOODHOUNDS, INC. · by Bill Myers
Hilarious, hair-raising suspense follows brother-and-sister detectives Sean and Melissa Hunter in these madcap mysteries with a message.

GIRLS ONLY! · by Beverly Lewis
Four talented young athletes become fast friends as together they pursue their Olympic dreams.

MANDIE BOOKS · by Lois Gladys Leppard
With over five million sold, the turn-of-the-century adventures of Mandie and her many friends will keep readers eager for more.

PROMISE OF ZION · by Robert Elmer
Following WWII, thirteen-year-old Dov Zalinsky leaves for Palestine—the one place he may still find his parents—and meets the adventurous Emily Parkinson. Together they experience the dangers of life in the Holy Land.

THE RIVERBOAT ADVENTURES · by Lois Walfrid Johnson
Libby Norstad and her friend Caleb face the challenges and risks of working with the Underground Railroad during the mid–1800s.

TRAILBLAZER BOOKS · by Dave and Neta Jackson
Follow the exciting lives of real-life Christian heroes through the eyes of child characters as they share their faith with others around the world.

THE YOUNG UNDERGROUND · by Robert Elmer
Peter and Elise Andersen's plots to protect their friends and themselves from Nazi soldiers in World War II Denmark guarantee fast-paced action and suspenseful reads.

*(ages 8–13)

Madcap Mysteries With a Message!

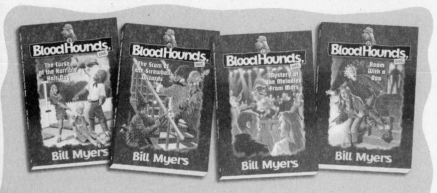

Strange things are afoot in the town of Midvale, and BLOODHOUNDS, INC. is on the case. A detective agency formed by Sean and Melissa Hunter, along with their bloodhound, Slobs, BLOODHOUNDS, INC. is on the trail of ghosts, wizards, UFOs, and other strange and seemingly supernatural things. But do these things really exist? Or are the bad guys trying to scare people?

With a deep trust in God's protection and some keen investigating, these two teens help bring the bright light of truth into some scary places. Terrific thrills and fast-paced fun make this an awesome set of stories!

1. *The Ghost of KRZY*
2. *The Mystery of the Invisible Knight*
3. *Phantom of the Haunted Church*
4. *Invasion of the UFOs*
5. *Fangs for the Memories*
6. *The Case of the Missing Minds*
7. *The Secret of the Ghostly Hot Rod*
8. *I Want My Mummy*
9. *The Curse of the Horrible Hair Day*
10. *The Scam of the Screwball Wizards*
11. *Mystery of the Melodies From Mars*
12. *Room With a Boo*

The Leader in Christian Fiction
◊BETHANYHOUSE